Janice Lynn has a Masters in Nursing from Vanderbilt University, and works as a nurse practitioner in a family practice. She lives in the southern United States with her husband, their four children, their Jack Russell—appropriately named Trouble—and a lot of unnamed dust bunnies that have moved in since she started her writing career. To find out more about Janice and her writing visit janicelynn.com.

Also by Janice Lynn

The Nurse's Baby Secret
The Doctor's Secret Son

Christmas in Manhattan collection

Sleigh Ride with the Single Dad
by Alison Roberts
A Firefighter in Her Stocking

And look out for the next books
The Spanish Duke's Holiday Proposal
by Robin Gianna
The Rescue Doc's Christmas Miracle
by Amalie Berlin
Available May 2018
Christmas with the Best Man
by Susan Carlisle
Navy Doc on Her Christmas List
by Amy Ruttan
Available June 2018

Discover more at millsandboon.co.uk.

A FIREFIGHTER IN HER STOCKING

JANICE LYNN

MILLS & BOON

First published in Great Britain 2017
by Mills & Boon, an imprint of HarperCollins*Publishers*
1 London Bridge Street, London, SE1 9GF

Large Print edition 2018

© 2017 Harlequin Books S.A.

Special thanks and acknowledgement
are given to Janice Lynn for her contribution to
the Christmas in Manhattan series

ISBN: 978-0-263-07266-2

MIX
Paper from
responsible sources
FSC www.fsc.org FSC® C007454

To James Mills, FDNY EMS Battalion 8,
and to Andrew Floied, Manchester Fire Rescue.
Thank you for your invaluable insight
and for being real-life heroes!

Any mistakes are my own.

CHAPTER ONE

IT WASN'T EVERY morning that Dr. Sarah Grayson stepped out of her apartment and saw a couple making out.

It had happened, though.

Same man, different woman.

Nausea churned in Sarah's belly. She ordered her eyes away, but since a nice, but somewhat bland apartment building corridor offered nothing to snag her attention, her gaze stayed put.

Making out in her hallway might be a bit of a stretch. Still, the couple stood in her rather hunky neighbor's apartment doorway, sharing a far from innocent kiss.

Even if the kiss had been a mere lip peck, her neighbor's lean hips wrapped in only a towel knocked innocent right out of the ball park. Home run.

Grand slam.

Sarah ran her gaze over his chiseled torso. He

rated pin-up-worthy—centerfold, for sure. Part of her couldn't blame the busty brunette for clinging to his broad shoulders. Or for totally ignoring the fact Sarah had stepped into the hallway. Common decency said they should pull apart and look a little embarrassed, right?

When Sarah's gaze collided with piercing blue ones, her breath caught. No embarrassment in those magnificent eyes. Just pure unadulterated sexual temptation.

Good grief. He probably was a grand slam.

What eyes. A color so intense they pulled you in and made you feel as if you were drowning, made you want to drown in everything promised in the enticing blue depths.

Not Sarah, of course.

She was immune to playboys like this guy. She'd built up her defenses years ago while listening to her mother harp about the blight of good-looking, fast-talking men.

Adulthood had fortified her defenses.

Still, she wasn't blind. Her neighbor was hot. She knew it and so did he.

Even as his lips lingered on the brunette's, those eyes crinkled with bad-boy amusement. Probably laughing at the fact Sarah had taken up full-fledged voyeurism.

Gaze locked with hers, he pulled back from the kiss.

"Baby," the brunette protested, still not noticing Sarah as she tugged downward on her cocktail dress skirt.

Good, the skimpy material barely covered her perfectly shaped bottom. A sticking plaster would cover more than the clingy sparkling spandex. Then again, if Sarah had curves like the brunette maybe she'd wear shrink-wrapped clothes, too.

She doubted it, but who knew? Sarah dressed to avoid drawing attention so she could focus on more important things than meaningless ogling. Either way, she'd never know because her stick-straight slender body lacked the brunette's hourglass shape.

"Brandy, we have company," her neighbor said, much in the way a parent would to a petulant child.

The brunette turned, flashing big almond eyes, raked her gaze over Sarah's shapeless body beneath her heavy jacket, scarf, and hat. She dismissed Sarah's importance and quickly turned back to towel boy.

He was better to look at than a ready-to-face-the-chill-of-a-Manhattan-November-early-morning Sarah.

Or Sarah on any morning, really.

"Jude," the woman practically cooed.

So that was his name. Jude.

He'd tried talking to her a few times when they'd bumped into each other in the hallway, but she'd ignored him. What would be the point? She wasn't interested in going through his revolving front door and he didn't seem the type to want to just be friends with a woman. Plus, he made her feel uncomfortable. Not a creepy uncomfortable, just a very aware of how male he was uncomfortable.

Realizing she was standing in the apartment hallway, gawking still, Sarah turned from the couple, locked her deadbolt, and pretended she couldn't hear Brandy begging to do anything he'd like her to do. Had the woman no pride?

Go home, girl. He used you.

Too bad Brandy's mother hadn't warned about men like him as Sarah's mother had repeatedly done.

At the woman's next words, Sarah's cheeks caught fire. Nope, no pride whatsoever.

Sarah turned and her gaze collided with

Jude's amazing blue one again. She'd swear those eyes could see straight into her very being, knew her thoughts. Maybe they even had some type of superpower because her stomach fluttered as if it had grown thousands of tiny wings.

Nausea, she told herself. Men like him made her sick. Out all hours of the night, never seeming to work, always with a different woman. Sick. Sick. Sick.

Maybe he was a gigolo or some kind of male escort.

Her nose curled in disgust to go along with her flaming cheeks.

"I think you've embarrassed my neighbor."

His voice was full of humor, which truly did embarrass Sarah. What was wrong with her? Standing in her hallway, as if frozen in place, ogling the man as if she'd never seen a bare chest.

She'd never seen one like his outside magazines and television, but that was beside the point.

She needed to get her voyeuristic self to work.

She couldn't make out most of what Brandy replied but caught the words "prude" and "dumpy". Ouch.

Refusing to look that way again, Sarah dropped her keys into the oversized bag she carried to work, and got out of Dodge before she had to listen to Jude's reply.

She hurried down the stairs, through the apartment complex foyer, and out onto the sidewalk to walk the few blocks to the hospital. The cold November wind bit at her face, but her jacket shielded her from the worst.

Too bad she'd not had a shield against what she'd just witnessed. That image was going to be hard to erase.

No doubt her neighbor had dismissed her as unimportant just as the brunette had. Sarah didn't care what he thought. Or what any man thought. She knew her strengths, her weaknesses. She preferred to be known for her brain and her heart rather than for outward appearances.

She was quite proud of who Sarah Grayson's brain and heart was. A dedicated emergency room doctor whom she believed made a difference in her patients' lives.

She wouldn't let her revolving bedroom door neighbor make her feel badly about herself. After all, what did he do?

He never seemed to do anything.

Except beautiful women.

On that, the man was an over-achiever.

A neighbor from the floor below said she thought he came from old money. Either Sarah was onto something with her paid male escort theory, or he was nothing more than a carefree, lecherous play-boy using his family to fund his depraved lifestyle.

Maybe she would get lucky and he'd move.

Adrenaline drove firefighter Jude Davenport as he pushed his way through the flame-filled building. Or maybe it was the heat that kept him moving. Sweat dripped down the back of his neck and his ears burned beneath his Nomex hood.

First checking temperature with his thermal im-aging camera, Jude opened a door and thick black smoke billowed out, banking low.

"Engine Seven to command. We are entering structure and making a left-hand search."

"Command copies Engine Seven is entering structure, making a left-hand search."

As lead man, Jude crawled to the left-hand wall and, staying in contact with him, his partner made his way around the room, using his axe to search. Visibility was next to nil thanks to the rolling black smoke.

They had to find her.

A four-year-old little girl was trapped in this hellish inferno.

Somewhere.

Along with more than a dozen tenants, they'd already rescued her mother and sister. Jude did not want to have to look that woman in the eyes and say he'd not been able to find her daughter.

He knew first-hand the pain of losing someone you loved and that drove him as he crawled toward a closed door he could barely make out.

A child was in there, was alive. Every instinct said she was.

He just had to get there, get to her, and pray that when he did find her, that she was still alive and he'd be able to get himself and her out of the fire.

Finally, he reached the door.

Then what he'd been dreading happened, what he'd known was coming because of how long they'd been searching in the burning building.

The air horn on the truck blew.

Once. Twice. Three long times.

"Command to all units. Evacuate the building. Repeat, evacuate the building."

He hadn't needed the sound of the horn or command coming over the radio speakers in his air pack to know things were bad and the building was lost.

Things were bad.

Somewhere in this hellhole was a terrified four-year-old.

"Command says part of the stairs has collapsed," his partner, Roger Woods, yelled. "We gotta go."

Jude had to check the room. They were too close to turn back without doing so.

"Seriously, Davenport," his partner called from behind Jude. "Don't make me drag your butt out."

"As if you could."

Roger was one of his best friends and Jude trusted the man implicitly. There was a reason Roger was his partner. Because they had similar life philosophies. They valued others' lives much more than their own. Roger wouldn't turn back any more than Jude would. Not when they were so close to where the girl was supposed to be.

Finally Jude got to the door. Using the back of his wrist and his thermal imaging camera, he checked the door for heat.

Hot, but not unbearable.

He reached up, grabbed the handle with his gloved hand, and opened the door.

The room wasn't quite as smoke-filled as the one he was leaving, but visibility was still barely above zero.

Reaching again for the camera hooked to the strap of his breathing apparatus, Jude scanned the room. The left and right walls glowed white, indicating that there was fire on both sides of the room. Jude was pretty sure the wall not lighting up, the opposite wall from him, was an exterior wall, which was good, because he was also pretty sure they weren't going out the way they'd come in.

Then, with the aid of the TIC cutting through the smoke and steam, the image of a little body not moving made his heart pound.

"Davenport? Do you hear me? Get out now," Command screamed in his ear.

It wasn't the first time Command had screamed at him.

He prayed it wasn't the last.

He didn't answer his boss. What was the point? He wasn't going anywhere. Not without the girl. He wouldn't leave her. He couldn't walk out of a burning building when the child's thermal image was in his sight. Reality was that Command wouldn't want him to. None of their crew would exit when a fire victim was within sight.

"There she is."

"Thank God," Roger called from behind him.

"Engine Seven to Command—we need a ladder to fourth division A-side window for rescue." God, he hoped there was a window on the exterior wall because he couldn't see a thing. "We have one victim."

Command acknowledged, repeating the call.

"Keeley?" Jude yelled, hoping the girl could hear him above the fire's loud roar. Hoping that she'd answer, that she'd move.

She didn't.

Please, don't let us be too late.

He couldn't see her with his bare eyes, but used the camera to guide himself toward her. The room was a sweltering hot box.

Then the thermal image on his TIC moved and Jude wanted to cry out in relief. She was alive. Who knew how much smoke she'd inhaled, what kind of burns she might have endured, but she'd moved so there was hope.

"Keeley," he called again, crawling toward her. "We're here to get you out of this place."

He had no idea if she could hear him over the deafening sound of the fire destroying the building. If she could, he wanted her to know he was on his way.

Finally, he reached the far corner of the room where she was huddled beneath her mother's bed.

Coughing, the little girl stared at him with watery eyes, but didn't make any move toward him or respond to his motioning for her to come to him. Was she asphyxiated?

In his gear, he couldn't fit under the huge low-rise bed she was hidden beneath and wasn't quite sure how he'd move the massive bed with her beneath it without risking hurting her, but he had to get to her fast. They had to get out of the building pronto.

"Keeley, we have to go." He tried again, tugging on the corner post of the solid wood monstrosity without any success. Was the thing nailed down? "Come to me, honey. Let me carry you out of this place."

"Don't leave me."

He could barely make out her words. Maybe he

even lip-read them more than heard them, but they rang loudly through his very soul.

As did the terror in her big puffy eyes as she coughed again.

"I won't leave you, Keeley. I promise. Crawl to me, Keeley." He purposely said her name over and over, hoping to get through to her, to let her know to come to him. He stretched his arms as far beneath the bed as he could. "Just move close enough that I can pull you to safety, Keeley, so we can get out of this building."

He heard a crash and knew another section of the structure had given way.

Any moment the building could come collapsing down.

They had to go now.

"Keeley, come to me," he pleaded, pushing against the bedpost again to see if it would move. Nope. The piece was solid, low to the floor, and heavy as hell.

He and Roger could stand, use their weight against the frame to see if they could shift it, and pray Keeley got out of the way if they did manage to move the massive piece of furniture.

She was crying, but she scooted forward a little, then back to where she'd been against the exterior wall.

Precious seconds were ticking by. Despite his protective gear, Jude could feel the worsening heat.

Instincts kicking in that said bad was about to get a whole lot worse if he didn't get her and get her now.

"I know it's scary, Keeley, but you're going to have to crawl to me so I can pull you to safety."

That was when she moved.

Finally.

"Just a little closer, Keeley." He reached as far as he could beneath the bed. "Just a little closer."

Then her hand touched his glove.

"That's it, Keeley. Just a little more."

His hand closed around her wrist and he pulled her to him.

"I've got her."

He wrapped his arms around her, just as a window burst out on the exterior wall.

Thank God. An exit.

No doubt the aerial truck platform was just outside the window and some of his guys were waiting to pull Roger, Keeley, and him through to safety.

Thank God.

"Don't leave me," the girl repeated, clinging tightly to him and then going limp in his arms.

"Never," he promised again, praying he'd not been too late.

Just as it had every day since the brown-out a couple of weeks before, the emergency room was hopping and had been all day. Sarah had run from one patient to the next with very little down time. Everything from having slipped due to ice to a gunshot wound had come through the doors.

Currently, she was examining a fifty-seven-year-old white male with chest pain and a history of triple bypass three years previously. The man admitted to smoking a pack a day for the past thirty years, drinking a pint a day, wasn't bothering to take his prescribed blood pressure and cholesterol medications, and was a good hundred pounds overweight. He had been a heart attack waiting to happen.

"Has your chest pain eased up, Mr. Brown?" she asked the clammy-looking man as she scanned back over the notes the nurse had made upon his arrival. He should have come by ambulance, but he'd walked into the emergency room.

"It has some," he said, squinting at her as if the light bothered his eyes. "But it's been hurting off and on for two days. This evening it got a lot worse and I couldn't catch my breath. This may just be another off spell."

His cardiac enzymes were running stat in the lab and his telemetry was showing a slight T-wave abnormality. She'd started him on a nitroglycerin drip and had called to have the cardiac cath lab readied.

"Has the shortness of breath gotten better since you started on the IV meds and oxygen?"

Although he still looked sweaty and pale, he nodded. "I am breathing easier."

If that labored mess was easier, she'd been right to call Cardiology. If the guy wasn't having a myocardial infarction, he was on the verge of a major cardiac event. She was sure of it.

"Hey, Sarah, we have incoming. House fire. Multiple victims. Most minor. One serious."

She cut her gaze toward the nurse who'd leaned into the emergency room bay. "Thanks, Shelley."

Sarah fought wincing. Burns, smoke inhalation,

and asphyxiation were all patients who gave Sarah nightmares. A few times during residency she'd gone home and wept at the absolute horribleness she'd witnessed. And she was seeing burn victims after the paramedics had done some clean-up.

She took a deep breath and turned back to her patient. "Mr. Brown, Dr. Andrews is on his way. He's going to take you to the cardiac lab to check your heart further by doing an arteriogram. I don't like how your EKG looks."

The man grimaced. "I had one of those a few years ago, after my bypass. They found some more blockages."

Not surprised, Sarah nodded, then turned as, on cue, Dr. Andrews stepped into the bay.

"Mr. Brown, this is Dr. Andrews." She heard a commotion outside the bay and knew the incoming fire victims had arrived. She nodded at the cardiologist, then at her patient. "I'm leaving you in capable hands."

With that she rushed to help, but came to an abrupt stop at what she saw when she stepped outside the bay.

The paramedics were rushing in a stretcher with an unconscious child wearing a facemask delivering oxygen. Keeping up with the stretcher, his dark brown hair matted to his head from sweat, dirt, and who knew what, was none other than her neighbor, talking to the little girl as if she were awake and hearing every word while he held onto her arm with his grimy hand.

He wore an NYFD uniform and looked like he'd just stepped out of a quick trip to hell.

CHAPTER TWO

SARAH'S CAREFREE, WOMANIZING, towel-wearing neighbor worked for the fire department?

So much for her male escort theory.

Mentally willing her paralysis away, she rushed to where the paramedics were rolling the unconscious girl and took a quick report.

"She was conscious when NYFD got to her, but went out just before they got her out of the building," the paramedic, Paul, informed while they rolled the girl into a bay. "She got a twenty-cc bolus of normal saline via her intraosseous line, and then at one hundred and fifty cc per hour."

He'd given the precise amount infused thus far, as knowing exact fluid replacement was crucial in a burn victim—especially a pediatric one.

"Also, morphine for pain at point four cc per kilogram." Paul grimaced. "Although lower than normal, her oxygen saturation has remained steady, going at one hundred percent, and there aren't any face burns, so maybe she won't need intubation, but we both know how quickly that can change."

Intubating a child if she didn't really need to was never something Sarah wanted to do. However, waiting until an urgent need arose wasn't either. Edema from the smoke and toxins inhaled could make getting the tube into the airway almost impossible. If the girl's lungs were swelling, the quicker she got intubated, the easier the feat would be accomplished.

Looking at the child, Sarah knew she'd be intubating.

"Gag reflex still present?"

"As of two minutes ago, yes," Paul answered.

"Get a warming blanket on her stat," Sarah told a nurse, disinfecting her hands and gloving up as she did so. "Were you able to get all her clothing removed?"

"Had to wet down the area on her right side, but otherwise her clothes came off fairly easily. Most of the burns are superficial, except that one and her hands."

Sarah nodded, and lifted the thin sheet to run her gaze over the girl's body. First-and second-degree burns on her arms and neck. A third-degree on her right torso and hands.

Sarah's heart squeezed.

Injured children were her least favorite aspect of her job. Every protective instinct inside her cried out at the injustice of a hurt child.

"Sorry, man, but you're going to have to step back," Paul told her neighbor as the paramedic bumped into him on the opposite side of the stretcher from Sarah.

Her neighbor didn't budge. "I told you, I promised Keeley I wouldn't leave her and I'm not going to."

His tone said they'd have to call Security to have him forcibly removed. He'd let go of the girl's arm when Sarah had inspected her burns, had been holding onto one of the few areas on the girl's arms that hadn't had burns, but he'd quickly taken hold again, as if he needed to be touching the child to let her know he was still there. Was the child someone he knew?

Sarah didn't want to deal with a commotion that might slow down Keeley's care. Plus, the thought of her neighbor being dragged out of her emergency department didn't sit well.

"I may need to ask him something about her injuries." Doubtful, but it sounded better than admitting she didn't want him forced to leave. "Let him stay."

Which was when Jude turned that blue gaze to her, really noticing her for the first time since entering the emergency room. Recognition immediately shone in his red-rimmed eyes.

Sarah's heart slammed against her ribcage like a ball bouncing around in a pinball machine, lights and bells going off all through her insides.

The absolute difference in Jude's appearance from the carefree, towel-wrapped sex god standing in his apartment doorway early that morning to this concerned, dirty, smelly firefighter determined to stay by a child's side messed with her mind. Could she have been so wrong? Was it even possible there was more to her sexy neighbor than met the eye?

Had recognition not lit in those amazing blue eyes of his she'd have sworn he must be a twin.

Part of her felt she should say something, to acknowledge him in some way during that millisecond moment of recognition. Instead, she returned her attention to where it belonged, on the unconscious girl.

The weird flutter in her stomach was back and on high speed.

Indigestion, she told herself. *It's just indigestion.*

Although she'd lived next to his apartment for several months, Jude hadn't paid a lot of attention to his next-door neighbor.

She kept to herself and barely acknowledged him, even when he'd tried talking to her a couple of times when she'd first moved in.

Honestly, until that morning, when he'd really looked at her for the first time, he'd have guessed her to be a lot older than the thirty or so she was.

She dressed much older, acted much older, and had never even glanced his way, much less made eye contact before today.

Not that she necessarily was dressed older now, more just dressed to hide whatever was beneath.

She wore hospital-issue scrubs in a faded gray color that hung on her body much as sackcloth would, leaving her shapeless, plain, and, at first look, a bit drab.

Interesting, because, as he'd noticed that morning, she had really great eyes behind those hideous monstrosities posing as glasses. She should seriously consider investing in contact lenses.

She had good skin and amazing cheekbones, too. He'd dated models who'd gone under the knife for cheekbones that weren't nearly as impressive.

Not that his neighbor did a thing to accent them. Mainly, it seemed her goal was to hide every God-given physical attribute she'd been blessed with. Why? Why would a young, healthy woman underplay herself?

Because she was a doctor and wanted to be taken seriously? Or had something happened in her past that had made her not want men to notice her physically?

Why did it even matter how she dressed and what had made her choose to do so?

All that flashed through his mind in the half-second his gaze connected with hers and recognition hit.

Some other emotion punched him in the gut, too, but he figured that was exhaustion, worry, and adrenaline battling around for dominance.

"Thank you," he told her for giving him the okay to stay, not that he'd been going to leave.

Short of interfering with Keeley's care, he'd have stuck by her side.

Just as he had after he'd made it out of the building and back to the ground, Jude had ignored the exhaustion in his own body, ignored his boss's insistence that he get himself checked out and tended to, and had stayed with the child.

Just as he'd stayed with her in the ambulance.

Had Paul not been the paramedic in charge that might not have flown, but fortunately his friend had been.

If only he could have found Keeley a few minutes quicker.

Thank God they'd gotten out when they had because his instincts hadn't been wrong.

Within seconds of their clearing the building, one of the outer walls and the remainder of the roof had caved in.

Had they not already been outside the inferno, they wouldn't ever have been.

A sobering thought.

"Jude, man, step back," Paul said, grabbing Jude's arm. "Let the doctor check her patient."

"Seriously, he can stay," his neighbor repeated, then began examining Keeley while the paramedic gave her further run-down on what had happened and the girl's objective findings and care while in the ambulance.

Without pausing in her examination, his neighbor gave the nurse more orders. Then, without turning to Jude, she asked him, "You are who saved her from a burning building?"

He tried not to let her incredulousness as she'd said "you", as if she didn't believe him capable of anything of the sort, get to him.

Watching as she parted Keeley's eyelids and shone a light into her eyes, checking her pupil reflexes, he shrugged. "Just did my job."

Although not as well as he should have because he should have found her sooner. If he had, her little body might not be marred from burns from who knew what she'd done prior to hiding underneath her mother's bed. She wouldn't be unconscious, wouldn't have needed the trip to the emergency room by ambulance. If only they could have gotten her out when they'd gotten the other tenants of the building, when they'd gotten her mother and sister out.

"Ha, don't let him fool you." Paul spoke up,

gesturing to Jude and not stopping, despite Jude's shake of his head in hopes of silencing his friend.

"He should have been wearing a cape today, because everyone had already been ordered out of the building. He just didn't listen. Never does." Paul shook his head. "First one in, last one out."

"An adrenaline junkie, eh?" his neighbor asked, still not looking his way. She checked Keeley's gag reflex and continued with her assessment.

The weight of his uniform suddenly pulled at his shoulders as he went to shrug again, making the movement require a lot more effort than it should have. He was tired. So tired.

"Or someone who couldn't live with himself if he left a kid in a burning building," he heard himself admit.

Besides, there was no one waiting on him to come home to prevent him from taking risks. He purposely kept his relationships simple. Had never been tempted to do otherwise.

Not since Nina.

His neighbor's gaze lifted to his and something shifted in her blue-green eyes, giving them the effect of shimmering sea water behind her glasses.

Oh, hell.

Maybe he'd inhaled too many fumes, too.

Or maybe it was because he'd just thought of Nina.

Whatever the cause, his head spun and he felt off kilter.

Way off kilter.

Like he might have to sit down.

He probably did need to rehydrate and replenish electrolytes. He'd sweated a bucket in that inferno and his uniform clung to him like a second skin, as did his sweat-smashed helmet hair.

That's why he felt dizzy.

Not because of whatever the odd emotion in— he glanced at her name badge—Dr. Sarah Grayson's eyes had been.

Rather than say anything further to him, she gave more orders to the nurse, ordering tests and treatments and things that were vaguely familiar but went far beyond Jude's basic first-aid skills.

"I need to intubate stat," she told the nurse. "She has internal swelling that's going to get worse. We need to act now before her airway becomes too swollen to get the tube down."

She said what size intubation tube she wanted and what anesthetic she'd like Keeley to be given

to ease the discomfort of having the line introduced down her throat and into her lungs. If the
girl regained consciousness, she wouldn't want it
to be due to discomfort while being intubated.

As if she'd predicted what was about to happen,
Keeley's oxygen saturation dropped several points
and the monitor alarm sounded.

Everyone hurried, setting up trays, responding
to whatever Sarah told them to do. A nurse asked
Jude to step back and he did so, knowing he was
in the way while holding Keeley's arm.

Letting the girl's wrist go left him feeling be-
reft. As long as he'd been feeling the warmth of
her skin, he could tell himself she was going to be
okay, that he hadn't been too late.

Exhausted, but running on adrenaline, Sarah went
to the private waiting area where she'd had a nurse
bring Jude hours ago.

The emergency room had calmed down just
enough for Sarah to take a much-needed break.
She'd suspected her neighbor would still be in the
small private lounge, waiting until he was allowed
to see the girl in the pediatric intensive care unit

where Sarah had transferred her to once she'd established an airway and stabilized the girl.

Thank God she'd gotten the line in on the first try. Keeley's lung tissue had already swollen and Sarah had felt the extra resistance.

She'd checked on the girl's mother and younger sister, who'd also been checked into the emergency department. Apparently, they'd gotten out of the fire much earlier than Keeley as their injuries had been minor and they'd arrived by private car.

The young mother had been allowed to see Keeley for a few minutes, then the worn-out woman and her toddler daughter had left the hospital with a friend as her businessman husband spent a lot of time working overseas.

Sarah couldn't imagine what the mother was going through, to have lost her home, her things, and to have almost lost one of her daughters.

The woman had just left and, although Keeley wasn't allowed visitors, Sarah planned to let Jude see the girl if he was still there.

A firefighter? Who would have believed the sexy man she lived next door to was an everyday hero who risked his life to save others?

Not her that morning, for sure.

Good grief, he could have been killed.

Paul, one of her favorite paramedics, had later brought in a pedestrian who'd been hit by a taxi. He'd gone on and on about his buddy Jude and what a real-life hero he was.

A real-life hero who was apparently as dog-tired as she was.

Stretched out in a chair, his eyes closed, Sarah took advantage of the opportunity to freely look at him.

As much as was possible for someone as unbelievably handsome as he was, he looked awful. His hair was matted to his head. He reeked of smoke and sweat and dirty man. His heavy overcoat was in the chair next to the one he slept in.

He needed a shower.

Which, of course, brought her brain back to that morning when he'd been squeaky clean and wrapped in a towel.

She closed her eyes.

No. No. No.

She did not want that image in her mind. Not now. Not when she looked at him and saw a man who'd risked his life to save a little girl.

Not when she saw someone who might have substance beneath those chiseled abs.

She didn't want to like him.

He was a playboy.

Then again, maybe he went through so many women because of not wanting to get into a serious relationship due to his high-risk job.

No, she corrected herself again. No. No. No. She was not going to make excuses for his womanizing ways.

Wasn't going to happen.

Only then he opened his eyes and caught her staring.

The intensity in his baby blues warned she might make lots of excuses for this man.

CHAPTER THREE

"KEELEY," JUDE SAID, fighting a yawn as he sat up in the waiting-room chair.

Even as hyped up as he'd been from the fire search and rescue, he couldn't believe he'd fallen asleep. Then again, searching a burning building drained a man from the anxiety, the adrenaline, the extreme heat, the sweat. Sometimes after a rescue he'd feel so tired he thought he might sleep a week.

"Is she still alive?" He prayed so. He'd gotten to her as quickly as he could. He knew that. But sometimes as quick as a person could just wasn't enough.

"Yes, she's stable," his neighbor told him from where she stood a few feet away. "It was touch and go for a short bit due to her pulmonary edema, but she responded to the medications and is holding her own."

He let out a sigh of relief. "Thank you."

Looking more than a little tired herself, Sarah

sank into the chair opposite him and stared across the few feet separating them.

Which gave him the opportunity to study her face full on.

She really did have amazing eyes. And great cheekbones.

Her lips were full and perfectly bowed. Kissable.

Where had that thought come from?

"Actually, all the thanks go to you. I shudder to think what would have happened if you hadn't found her."

He knew what would have happened and that was why he did his job. He loved being a firefighter. Not that he could save every person, but he gave it his best. Always.

"Every firefighter's nightmare. Not finding someone," he admitted, raking his fingers through his matted hair. "The kind of stuff that messes with your head."

Maybe he should have gone home, showered, then come back. He supposed that would have been better than passing out in a private waiting area. Yet he'd not been able to leave. Not until he'd known Keeley was okay.

Sarah's plump lower lip disappeared between

her teeth for a brief second, and then she asked, "Does it mess with your head, Jude?"

Her saying his name for the first time messed with his head.

Big time.

Which made no sense.

As hadn't the fact he found her lips kissable.

She wasn't the type of woman he messed around with. He preferred women who knew the score and were okay with that. Dr. Sarah Grayson didn't seem the one-night-stand kind.

Yet he'd be lying if he didn't admit there was something about her that appealed to him in a major way.

Must be the day he'd had and that despite the fact he'd chugged a couple of sports drinks, he still felt dry to the bone.

"Some days more than others," he answered.

Today, for instance, everything was getting to him. The woman sitting across from him had intrigued him that morning.

She intrigued him now.

The in between had been a living hell and maybe she was an angel sent to redeem him.

Lord knew, he needed redeeming.

"Like today?" She read his mind.

He shrugged. "You trying to map out my psyche on the DSM-V, Doc?"

At his question, her brow arched. Then she offered up a small smile and it was as if the sun had come out on a cloudy day.

"I'm not that type of specialist," she pointed out, the light shining in her eyes saying he wasn't going to get a further answer to his question. "Do you want to see Keeley?"

"Can I?" He hadn't expected to get to see the child. Not tonight when she was still so critical. He'd stayed to find out how she was and had then dozed off in exhaustion.

Odd, at the moment he felt oddly refreshed. Which was absolutely crazy because he was starved, dehydrated, and grimy as hell. He probably smelled like he'd been there, too.

Most of the women he knew would have been pinching their noses and ordering him to shower. Then again, most of the women he knew liked the wealthy Davenport side of him more than the real him firefighter side.

His neighbor didn't currently look bothered by his physical state one way or the other. But that morning, when she'd raked those sea-green eyes over him, she'd been bothered. He'd seen it in the way she'd swallowed hard, in the way her pulse had throbbed at her throat just above her loose scarf, in the way she'd nervously wet her lips.

Sweet heavens, she'd just gulped and licked her lips again.

Which meant what exactly? He wasn't sure. That she found him physically distracting even when he was a mess?

Why did that possibility make him feel all he-man?

"Isn't seeing Keeley what you've waited for?" She answered his question with one of her own.

"Either that or I just needed a quick nap to regain my strength."

"Busy night ahead?" Her sarcasm couldn't have been more obvious if she'd taken out a billboard.

"Aren't they all?" he answered, gauging her response. That he'd confused her was apparent on her lovely face.

She watched him from narrowed eyes. "If I didn't already know the answer, I'd ask if you ever take anything seriously. Thanks to this evening, I know you do."

"I should set the record straight, then. I only joined the fire department to get women."

Her cheeks turned a bright pink, then she gave him a disgusted, *I knew it* look. "I figured as much."

Jude stifled a chuckle at her defensive arm-crossing and chin-lifting. "Are you saying you think I'm shallow, Sarah?"

Cheeks still glowing, she rolled her eyes. "You like to tease, don't you?"

Not since Nina.

The thought blindsided him and he almost grimaced, but kept from doing so at the last second. No way was he letting thoughts of Nina into his head again today. Not now. Not at the hospital.

Not when his doctor cousin, Charles, could be around.

So, instead of letting his mind go to the past, he focused on the woman sitting across from him, grateful for the fire in her eyes.

"I'd be lying if I didn't admit to liking how you respond." He did like her intelligence, her quick wit, that spark in her eyes. He was used to being physically attracted to women. Women were beautiful creatures. But with Sarah the attraction was something more than her gorgeous eyes and amazing cheekbones. The flash in those eyes was what drew him in, made him want to know more about the woman beneath the deceptive outer layer.

A want he hadn't felt since…nope, he wasn't going to think of her.

"Why?" Sarah asked, studying him as if he were some gross bug under a magnifying glass.

"Why not?"

"Because I'm not one of your women."

He wouldn't pretend he didn't know what she meant. Hadn't he just been thinking the same thing a few moments before?

His women lived in the moment, were experienced in the ways of the world, and were no more interested in anything beyond immediate pleasure than he was.

Unlike the scowling woman sitting across from him.

The scowling woman whose smile had lit up dark corners of his very being, an addictive feeling he'd like to sample again.

Although some dark corners might be best left in the shadows.

Unable to resist teasing her further, he waggled his brows. "Would you like to be?"

Her jaw dropped. "No!"

He gave a low laugh at her outrage. "That was quick. I think I'm offended. Is it my cologne?"

"Right." She glared. "Because you're so easily offended that a woman saying no just breaks your heart."

She might be saying no, but her eyes were singing an entirely different tune. They were shooting fire of feminine awareness. Interesting.

"Sure you don't want to think about it?" he teased, enjoying the blush in her cheeks.

"Positive. Some things a girl just knows."

"Yeah?" He arched his brow. "There's some things a woman just knows, too."

Her gaze searched his and her voice cracked a little when she asked, "Such as?"

"How she responds to a man." There were definitely sparks flying back and forth. He might have had a rough day but he wasn't hallucinating the energy between them.

Not that he understood the chemistry, but he'd have to be brain dead not to recognize the man-woman pull.

"Don't go confusing me with one of your bimbos," she warned, chin notching upward. "I'm not interested in a guy like you."

"A guy like me? Oh, yeah." He grinned, refusing to be insulted. "We established that I'm shallow."

Her gaze narrowed further, but the outraged look wasn't working. Not when her lips twitched.

"I didn't call you shallow," she pointed out.

"You didn't correct me."

"Because you weren't wrong," she countered.

He arched his brow.

Rather than answer, she jumped up from the chair and gave him an expectant look. "Do you or do you not want to see Keeley with me?"

Standing, he grinned. "I most definitely want to see Keeley with you, Doc."

Her hands went to her hips. "Don't call me that."

"Why not?" He kind of liked the nickname. It fit. Plus, she needed a nickname to lighten her up a bit. "It's as good a nickname as any."

"You don't need a nickname for me."

"Sure I do, so I can call it out when you're ninja-ing in and out of your apartment."

"Ninja-ing?"

"That thing you do where you come and go and hope no one sees."

"Whereas you hang around in the hallway long enough to make sure everyone sees you in your God-given glory?"

Lord, he loved her sharp wit, that whatever he threw out, she had a quick response. "Does that bother you?"

"Of course not. You can do whatever you want. In your apartment. With your bimbos."

"They aren't bimbos."

"They're not bright and upstanding citizens."

"For all you know about them, they could be."

"I know they spent the night with a man who used them so that checks bright right off their list of attributes."

"Sex for mutual pleasure isn't my using them any more than it is their using me."

"So it's a case of mutual using and that somehow makes it okay? Keep fooling yourself if you want, but there are some of us smart enough to know better."

He was standing so close to her now that he was looking straight down into her eyes, was tempted to remove her glasses so he could more fully see into their depths.

"I suppose a really pessimistic, prudish person might see mutual pleasure that way." He egged her on, liking the spark his words elicited.

"And who are you? Mr. Optimism? Going around spreading happiness and cheer?" she scoffed with an exaggerated eye roll. "More like spreading something else with how many different women I've seen come out of your apartment."

His lips twitched. "You keeping tabs?"

"Hardly, but I'm not blind."

Arguable with those ugly glasses she wore.

"For the record, I'm not spreading anything." He wanted the record straight. He wouldn't let himself delve into why it mattered, but he needed her to know the truth. "I'm a safety kind of guy. Always."

"Who runs into burning buildings when everyone else is running out? Yeah, try selling me another one."

"Someone has to do it."

Her chin tilted upward and her gaze didn't waver behind the thick glasses. "Good thing there's you."

"Yeah, good thing."

* * *

A bone-weary Sarah ninja-ed down the hallway and stealthily let herself into her apartment, pausing in her open doorway to glance at Jude's closed door.

So much had happened since that morning when he'd been standing in that doorway.

He'd been flirting with her at the hospital.

She should have checked him for hypoxemia-induced psychosis related to smoke inhalation.

Because no way was he in his right mind.

Or maybe it was her who wasn't in her right mind.

Maybe she'd accidentally inhaled some anesthesia or hallucinogenic medication that was messing with her head.

Something was messing with her head.

More like someone.

Because Jude's teasing and hot looks refused to leave her mind even long after he'd left the hospital.

For the rest of her shift and an hour into the next when she'd stayed to help catch up the overload of patients, she'd battled with the facts that Jude was a womanizer, an incurable flirt, heroic when he'd rushed into a burning building to save Keeley, and sweet when he'd waited at the hospital.

Heroic. Sweet. Not adjectives she'd have ever thought she'd attach to the incorrigible towel-wearing man from that morning.

Unable to stop herself, she glanced toward his closed apartment door again. Was he home?

Should she check on him, make sure he was all right, that the smoke truly hadn't gotten to him, that he'd rehydrated well?

Then again, he might not be alone and the absolute last thing she wanted was to see Jude Davenport with another woman twice in the same day.

Especially after he'd so blatantly flirted with her.

Especially after, despite her best attempts not to, she'd so blatantly liked his flirting.

So, her neighbor had a few redeeming qualities.

That didn't mean they should become friends or have anything to do with one another.

They shouldn't.

Best thing she could do was forget today had even happened and stay far, far away from the man at all costs.

Determined that she was going to do exactly that, Sarah quietly closed her apartment door.

She was going to shower, eat whatever she could find and quickly prepare, sleep, and not think about her neighbor.

After he'd left the hospital, Jude had returned to the fire hall, showered, filled out appropriate paperwork, then come home to make himself something to eat.

He'd had plans with friends, but had opted to cancel, deciding he'd rather have a simple meal at home, a glass of wine, relax, and enjoy his apartment's amazing view of the city he loved so much.

Jude enjoyed cooking, enjoyed throwing ingredients together that pleased his senses and filled his stomach. He'd never been formally trained, but was pretty good. Even Nina had thought so.

Nina. She'd snuck into his thoughts too often today. Why?

Then again, thinking he could go to the hospital where Charles worked and not think of his cousin's late wife was foolish. After all, hadn't Jude introduced the woman he had been in love with to his cousin and she'd fallen head over heels for the emergency room doctor instead?

That Nina had fallen for Charles, rather than

Jude, had never sat well, had ruined his friendship with Nina and left him on edge around his
cousin. That feeling hadn't gone away after Nina
and Charles had married. If anything, it had gotten worse.

Nina trying to repair the damage to their friendship hadn't helped. Feeling betrayed, angry, Jude
had refused to have anything to do with her. They'd
fought and never spoken again.

Nina's heartbreaking death due to complications
from giving birth to twins had left an inconsol-
able hole in Jude's heart that bled anew every time
he saw Charles so he avoided him. Grief, guilt,
anger, so many emotions ran rampant when his
past collided with the present. Thankfully, he'd
not bumped into his cousin during the hours he'd
been at the hospital waiting on news of Keeley.

Which brought his mind back to who he had
bumped into at the hospital.

His uptight neighbor.

Confusing, plain Jane Sarah Grayson who wasn't
really so plain beneath her attempts to appear to
be.

An emergency room doctor.

Like Charles.

ling the baking dish out of his oven with a
older, Jude lifted the lid and made a small
into the chicken. Almost done. Another fif-
n minutes or so and it would be perfect.

Restless from thoughts of Nina, of his intrigu-
g neighbor, from life, Jude walked into his liv-
ig room, meaning to stand at his floor-to-ceiling
glass windows to stare out at the New York City
skyline.

Instead, he frowned and strained to figure out
what the noise was that he could barely make out.

Then it hit him.

A smoke alarm was going off in the unit next
to his.

Sarah's apartment.

CHAPTER FOUR

How could an intelligent woman who could save lives not cook a simple piece of toast without burning it?

Okay, Sarah didn't usually burn her food, but this wasn't the first time. But she didn't recall ever doing so to the point that her alarm went crazy.

How did she get the thing to go off?

Pulling the plug on the toaster oven, she closed the door, rushed to where the alarm blared over the doorway. The baggy sleeve of her way oversized sweatshirt flopped as she fanned a dishtowel back and forth, hoping it would clear the smoke and shut the thing up.

"Stop that," she ordered the shrill bell, dancing around beneath it as she waved the towel with gusto and thought about how much she detested cooking. Almost as much as she detested this horrible alarm. "Stop. Stop. Stop."

Was she going to have to call Maintenance? Or

they just automatically showed up when the apartment's smoke alarms went off?

ud knock pounded at her apartment door.

l, that answered that. Maintenance had just n up.

iich was a good thing since her fanning wasn't :ing.

ily when, flustered, she flung her front door i, Maintenance wasn't who stood there.

ne man she'd been thinking about not thinking out stood there, wearing jeans, a plain white V-icked T-shirt, and nothing on his feet.

Good grief. He'd metamorphosed back into a exy beast.

Not that he hadn't been sexy at the hospital.

Clearly, he had, because he'd twitterpated her to the point of burning her toast and filling her kitchen with smoke.

His blue gaze raked over her, obviously satisfy-ing any doubts as to whether or not she was okay, and then he grinned. "Miss me?"

Pretending all was fine, that there wasn't a loud shrill screaming behind her, she wrinkled her nose at him, wishing she had on her glasses to shield herself from his probing gaze. "No."

Why on earth would he think she had? Before that morning, they'd never even made eye contact, much less spoken to each other.

His eyes danced with humor. "You sure about that?"

Wishing the stupid ear-piercing alarm would go silent so it would quit rattling her brain, she lifted her chin and stared straight into his eyes, thinking it very unfair that a man had his stunning eyes and long lashes. "Positive. Go away."

He laughed. "That's not the sound of your smoke alarm beckoning your friendly neighborhood firefighter your way?"

Oh. That's what he'd meant?

"No." If she looked sure enough, haughty enough, despite the obvious alarm blasting in the background, he'd take the hint and leave, right?

Nope.

Looking way too comfortable in his perfectly fitting jeans and just right chest-hugging T-shirt, he arched a thick masculine brow.

"Yes," she corrected, because, really, it wasn't as if he didn't recognize that annoying sound. Pretending otherwise just made her look foolish. "It is my smoke alarm, but it's not supposed to beckon you. Go home."

He shrugged as if it was no big deal, then asked, "You don't want me to turn off your alarm?"

"Could you, please?" she heard herself say, moving aside to let him into her apartment as if his words had been some secret magic phrase to grant entrance. "I can't get the thing to shut up."

His lips twitched. "If you ask nicely."

What? Her mouth fell open. Was he kidding her? But before she could come back with some retort, he came into her apartment and was following the smoke signals and noise to her kitchen.

When her gaze dropped to his jeans-clad butt that could sell millions of pairs of pants if someone would stick an ad up on a Times Square billboard, Sarah blamed the noise for interfering with her brain waves. No way would she have otherwise visually ogled the man's bottom, lit-up-billboard-worthy or not.

Within seconds, he'd pulled over a chair and climbed onto it. Looking like some sexy god up on his perch, he reset her smoke alarm.

Despite how much he annoyed her, the silence

had her wanting to wrap her arms around him in gratitude.

"Bless you!" she praised. "That thing was driving me crazy."

Turning, he stepped down from the chair and carried it back to where he'd grabbed it from. "No problem."

"How did you know?"

Facing her, hands on his narrow hips, he grinned. "Told you. I succumbed to the sound of your mating call."

She shook her head. Maybe in denial of his claim. Maybe in denial of memories of those hips wrapped in a towel and nothing more. Maybe in denial of the fact that for the first time in her life she was an ogler. She didn't like it. Not one bit.

Mating call. As if.

"I didn't lure you here," she choked out of her dry mouth. Seriously, her vocal cords felt like they'd been put through a dehydration machine.

His amusement apparent, he cocked a brow. "Really? You expect me to believe your smoke alarm accidentally set itself off on the same day you learned I'm a firefighter?"

It did sound fairly incredible.

"Admit it," he continued, his eyes dancing with mischief. "You wanted to see me and issued an invitation you knew I wouldn't refuse."

"I…" She grimaced. He made a good point. One that made any argument she issued lack credibility, even though she hadn't intentionally set off her smoke alarm. Neither had she wanted to see him.

Quite the opposite.

She'd seen him too much that day already.

Seen and liked. Even the dirty, worn-out endearing hospital version. Unfortunately.

Wincing, he took in the smoke still escaping from her toaster oven. "You didn't have to really set fire to anything, Sarah. A simple knock on my door and a verbal invitation would have done." He shrugged. "Or, if you wanted something more dramatic, a match next to that sensitive baby there would have had it screaming for me."

"I didn't…" She paused, flustered by his teasing, by how her heart pounded that he was there, inside her apartment, talking directly to her, that he was using the teasing flirty tone as he had at the hospital.

"Need rescuing?" He finished her sentence for her. He walked over to the toaster oven, opened the door, grimaced at the burned mess inside. "Sure you did. In more ways than one. What was that?"

"Toast."

His eyes widened. "That was toast?"

At his question, something inside Sarah snapped.

"Yes, it was. Toast. Toast that was going to be my dinner, because I was hungry and tired and... Don't you judge me...you...you..." She searched for a derogatory name, sure there were thousands just on the tip of her tongue. Unfortunately, none sprang forth.

That's when the day's events took their toll and she did something totally out of character.

She watered up and fought tears.

Uh-uh. No way.

She was not going to cry in front of him.

Not now. Not ever.

She was not going to cry period.

She did not cry and most certainly if she ever did it wouldn't be over burnt toast.

"Sarah?" His tone was no longer teasing, but showed concern. "Are you okay?"

Embarrassed, exhausted, ready to call it a night, she took a deep breath. "I'm tired and hungry and my dinner is chunks of charcoal and you annoy me. No big deal."

He eyed her way too closely for comfort.

"You were really going to have toast for dinner?" he asked, ignoring the rest of her comment.

"I was going to spread hummus on it," she defended. She'd showered, thrown on the baggy sweats, and had planned to eat a quick bite and crash. She did the same thing quite frequently on the days she worked the emergency room and got held up beyond her normal twelve-hour shift.

His nose curled again. "Hummus and toast. No, thank you."

"For your information, I like hummus and toast."

He didn't look convinced. "Your hummus and toast must be better than any I've ever had."

"It's good. Stick around and you can taste for yourself." Sarah heard herself say the words, but had no clue where they came from. Not in a million years would she invite her neighbor who started his days with a different woman every day of the week to stay for dinner.

Good grief. What would he think?

He had come to turn off her alarm, so she

couldn't really retract her invitation, could she? Not without seeming ungrateful and rude.

"Tempting," he ventured, not sounding anything of the sort. "But I have a better offer."

Of course he did. Women probably lined up to cook gourmet meals for him. And she'd heard first-hand that morning what else they offered.

"Why don't you come to my place and let me cook for you?"

Surprised, she opened her mouth to refuse, but he continued speaking before she could.

"Before you say no, the food is already in the oven, the wine is chilled, and I have a view that's even more amazing than yours."

He'd noticed her view? He had food in the oven? Why did he have wine chilling?

Then it hit her.

"I pulled you away from company, didn't I?"

He frowned. "No. Why would you think that?"

Because his apartment door was like a model runway exit, always with some beautiful woman walking through it.

But his look said he'd been alone.

"You're cooking for just yourself?"

"I like to eat."

Wondering at his apartment view, at what he'd cooked and how edible it was, she eyed him suspiciously. "What's the catch?"

"No catch. Just offering to share my dinner." He glanced toward the burned remains of her toast. "And looking out for my own interests of having an uninterrupted meal, of course. I don't want you attempting more toast and setting your alarm off again."

"Ha-ha. Real funny. The only reason my toast caught fire is because I was so tired." And had been distracted by thoughts of him, but she wasn't telling him that part.

"Fine. You can take a cat nap on my sofa while I finish up dinner."

As if.

"What are you serving?" she ventured out of curiosity, but with no intention of even entertaining the possibility of actually agreeing to have dinner with him. "I might prefer burnt toast."

He laughed and shook his head. "You won't. We're having Chicken Marsala served on a bed of angel-hair pasta, steamed asparagus with a light butter sauce, and a red wine because I prefer red to white."

Of course he did. Red stood for passion and white was just bland, right? Jude was a red kind of guy.

She blinked. "Are you for real?"

"You could pinch me and find out."

His eyes twinkled with that sparkle that had her heart doing funny floppy things in her chest.

"You wish."

Jude did wish.

As crazy as the thought was, he wanted Sarah to pinch him.

Not to see if he was real, but to wake him up because he was moving in some type of haze.

What was he thinking, inviting her to dinner? Not about how beautiful she was without her thick glasses blocking her face.

She was, but he was being a good neighbor.

That was it.

He wasn't inviting her to his place for anything more.

Even if she did have gorgeous eyes, amazing cheekbones, and full, pink, kissable lips.

"Is that how you lure women to your apartment? With promises of feeding them?"

"Something like that," he answered, wondering why she thought the worst of him when it came to women.

Maybe through her eyes, there were too many women, and maybe, if he was honest, he'd admit to it as well.

But he never deceived any of them or made promises he had no intention of keeping. They all knew the score. He was a one-night-stand kind of guy and the women he invited to his apartment came for one reason.

It wasn't so Jude could cook for them.

Sarah wasn't like the women he brought to his apartment for sex.

"I'm not interested in being lured to your apartment."

Suddenly feeling weary, restless, and as if maybe Sarah was right not to want to come to his apartment, he sighed. "I'm inviting you to my apartment to eat dinner." He put emphasis on the word. "You're tired. I'm tired. We've both had a long day. I want a good meal, to relax, and a good night's rest, Sarah. Nothing more. My invitation to feed you is with no strings attached and no hidden motives to trick you into my bed."

He'd never had any need to trick women into his bed. There was always one ready and willing to fill the empty spot in his life.

Tonight he'd just wanted to be alone.

Which didn't quite jibe with his burning desire for Sarah to say yes.

"Because I'm not your type?" she questioned, confirming his earlier thoughts.

"You're not my type." He meant to say more, to elaborate on the reasons why, to elaborate on the fact that she intrigued him and he'd like to let down her hair, see her smile, hear her laughter so he'd know what it sounded like, but her sigh of relief had him holding his tongue.

"Fine." She didn't sound or look happy about agreeing so the smile and laughter might not be forthcoming anytime soon. "In that case, I'll eat with you, but I'm eating, checking out this view you bragged about, and then I'm leaving, *capisce*?"

Sarah had bought her beloved apartment for three main reasons. Its walking distance proximity to Manhattan Mercy, it fitting within her budget, barely, and the spectacular view.

Just like the man, Jude's view really did blow her away.

As did his apartment.

At some point, someone had taken two, maybe three, apartments and converted them into one luxurious one. His living room dwarfed hers, as did the floor-to-ceiling views of the twinkling New York City nightlife. Just *wow*.

Forget needing food. She'd just sit here, sip on the glass of wine he'd given her to keep her occupied while he finished up their meal, stare out at the skyline, and soak up the energy of the busy city she adored, to revive her exhausted soul.

Having grown up in Queens in various dumpy housing projects, when they'd had a home, Sarah had great appreciation for how far she'd come, for the luxuriousness of her small apartment, and especially for the grandeur of the apartment she was currently in.

Listening to the soothing surround-sound music he'd turned on with the click of a remote control and a voice command, Sarah scanned the room. Simple, but high-quality furniture. Artwork that was probably originals. The gigantic remote control that seemed to control everything in the apartment. Jude lived way beyond a firefighter's salary.

Which meant he either came from money or had another, more lucrative side job.

For a moment, she let her mind again toy with the idea of him being a hired escort. Ha, if so, maybe she should consider his services for her upcoming holiday events so she didn't have to go by herself.

Not that she minded being single. Just that at certain events being solo stood out like a sore thumb. Like at engagement parties and weddings and various get-togethers with her coworkers.

Coworkers, which included her boss. Charles Davenport. Davenport. Jude Davenport.

Duh. How could she have been so blind?

The last name. The eyes. She'd not put two and two together, but her conclusion made perfect sense.

Jude's eyes were the same blue as her boss's.

His last name was also the same.

That couldn't be a coincidence.

No way.

He was one of those Davenports.

"You ready to eat crow?"

Startled by his question, she jerked toward him,

watching as he walked out of the kitchen, stepped up a step to where there was a table for four, and put down two plates.

Good grief, the man did things for a pair of jeans that ought to be declared illegal in every state but Alaska. Maybe there, it was cold enough to offset the burning heat that rose inside her every time she looked at him. *Wowzers.*

"Crow?" She arched a brow, grateful she'd forced her gaze up above his waistline as he turned toward her. "You told me you were serving chicken."

He grinned. "I meant the view. It's phenomenal, isn't it?"

Yeah, it was and she didn't just mean the New York City skyline. Seeing the eagerness with which he waited for her to respond, she marveled at the unexpected layer to him. He appreciated his view of the city that much?

That surprised her, made her have to admit there were more dimensions to Jude than she'd already realized.

She didn't need to discover any more positive dimensions. The fact he'd risked his life to save a young girl's already had her softening way too much.

That had to be why she was looking at him and feeling all warm and fuzzy on the inside.

Or maybe it was the wine.

She wasn't much of a drinker and she'd finished one glass and started another.

On an empty stomach.

Definitely that was it.

What had she been thinking?

No matter. Life was good.

"Haven't seen any crows, not even any pigeons this high up." She took another sip of the wine, despite just thinking that she should probably slow down or stop altogether. "But it's not bad."

He laughed. "You don't like admitting to being wrong, do you?"

She batted her lashes all innocent like. "What was I wrong about?"

"My view."

"I never said anything about your view," she reminded him, holding his gaze. "You were the one who said your view was better than mine. Not me."

"You're right," he conceded, then gestured to the view from where he stood on the raised platform dining area. The floor-to-ceiling windows behind him displayed a city that sparkled like diamonds under perfect lighting. "But, admit it, I'm also right."

She ran her gaze across the skyline, wondering if the city would ever fail to amaze. "You have an amazing view, Jude Davenport. Much better than mine, even. Happy?"

"Yes. Thank you. I am."

She tore her gaze away from the window and looked at him. With his easygoing smile, he actually did look happy. And relaxed. And way too handsome in his jeans, T-shirt, and bare feet.

The view she was looking at was better than any she'd seen in her apartment. A smiling gorgeous man gesturing to the Manhattan skyline. Yeah, that had never happened in her apartment.

For that matter, until tonight she'd never had a man in her apartment other than movers as she'd not wanted her few dates since moving in to taint her beloved home. She'd known with each one that things weren't going to work out. Maybe she was too picky, but better picky than ending up with some loser. Just ask her mother. Not that you had to ask. Sarah's mother vocalized the plague of society—men—to anyone and everyone who got within earshot.

That morning Jude had seemed to fit her mother's horror stories to a T. But firefighter Jude and this relaxed, easygoing, comfortable, bare-footed domesticated Jude refused to be shoved into that preconceived mold.

He wiggled his toes, as if knowing she was looking at them. Sarah wasn't a foot fetish kind of girl, or any kind of fetish girl, really, but there was something about this man's bare feet that she found appealing.

Maybe it wasn't the bare feet, but the entire package that was getting to her.

She gulped back a drink, then fought to keep from coughing as the sweet wine went down all wrong. That's all she needed, to aspirate, and choke in front of him. He'd think her a total klutz, having already set off her smoke detector.

Or that she'd purposely choked so he'd have to come to her rescue again.

When her gaze met his again, he was studying her as intently as she was him.

"I get the impression you really can see my view, Sarah."

Um, yeah, she could. His point was?

"Not once have I seen you squint," he continued. "Which makes me question those glasses you wear. It's going to be a tough sell to convince me you need them. Are they prescription?"

Busted.

"They serve their purpose."

His brow arched. "Which is?"

To put a barrier between her and anyone who tried to look too closely. As Jude was currently doing.

She should have grabbed them off her bathroom sink before heading to his place. She just hadn't been thinking clearly, and that had been way before she'd drunk any wine.

"Something smells wonderful. You sure I can't help?" she asked, needing to pull herself out of whatever trance he was putting her in.

"Positive." He came to stand by where she sat, held out his hand. "It's all done and on the table. Hungry?"

Being careful not to slosh her wine, she slipped her hand into his, not surprised one bit by the warmth, the tingles that zapped her at the skin-to-skin contact, the burning heat that settled deep in her belly.

It was only fitting that the man had the powers

of Zeus to shoot lightning bolts through unsus-
pecting women.

"Starved."

And not just for food.

Oops. There went the wine again.

CHAPTER FIVE

"YOU MAY HAVE ruined me to hummus and toast forever." Sarah patted her mouth with a napkin, then leaned back in her chair and smiled. "Shame on you, spoiling my rather dull palate."

Jude felt rather spoiled himself, having gotten to watch Sarah eat. And loosen up. Now, that he'd enjoyed.

Because once she'd relaxed she'd opened up and talked.

Sarah talking was a pleasure.

She fascinated him. From her political views to her dreading the holidays as much as he was to her fear of taking the tunnels out of the city to her absolute love of New York and the diversity of people, customs, restaurants, and things to do.

He couldn't quite believe she'd lived in New York her entire life and had never been to a Broadway show. How did anyone manage that? Even prior to adulthood, he'd repeatedly gone during prep school field day trips.

He leaned forward, pinning her with his gaze. "If you could see any one Broadway show, which one would it be?"

"Phantom of the Opera," she said without hesitation and with a wistful look in her eyes that even her hideous glasses wouldn't have hidden.

"Obviously, you've given this some thought. Why haven't you gone?"

Glancing away from him to stare out the window at the skyline, she shrugged. "I made plans to go once. He failed to show and I've just never made plans to go again."

He?

"What?" He exaggerated the word, a bit stunned at her reason. "Are you kidding me? Some guy stood you up?"

Meeting his gaze for a brief moment, she shook her head, then stared down into her glass, twirling the small amount of sparkling wine remaining. "I… It's okay, really."

"You were all dressed up and waiting on the guy to take you on a date and he never showed?" Maybe his question had been crass, but the possibility that some clown had blown her off just seemed unfathomable. And made him angry for her. He should get the guy's address and give him a lesson on how to treat a lady. Because, despite Sarah's denial, her voice conveyed that she'd been hurt.

As did how her eyes were downcast and her face pale.

"You were, weren't you?"

"I was what?" Her gaze lifted to his.

The glistening in her eyes almost undid him. She was fighting tears. His insides clenched as did his fingers.

"Dressed up and waiting on a man who never showed and didn't bother to let you know he wasn't coming."

Her expression pinched and that was all the answer Jude needed. Yeah, he should really look up this tool and give him a piece of his mind.

"Was he straight?"

Sarah's face turned that rosy shade of red it seemed to often wear and she nodded. "Yes, he was straight. Like I said, he just forgot we'd made plans."

"How?" If he'd exaggerated the word earlier,

this time was even more drawn out with total disbelief.

Looking embarrassed, Sarah shrugged. "You're making a big deal of it. It wasn't. He got busy and forgot about our date. It's fine. After that, we realized we weren't meant to date, but are still friends. End of story."

Only not really because the beautiful woman sitting across from him had taken a blow to her confidence that never should have happened. The thought of Sarah, all dressed up and waiting for her date, and the guy not bothering to show or call, had Jude livid.

He shook his head. "The guy stood you up and you're still friends with him? You should have kneed him where it hurt, not still be defending his bad-mannered behavior."

Eyes wide, she gave him a horrified look. "Why on earth would I do that? Because he and I didn't click romantically? That doesn't mean he's a bad person. He's not. He's a nice man."

Most of the women he knew would have neutered the guy, not defended him.

Wondering at why Sarah was, if she still had feelings for the idiot who'd stood her up, Jude shook his head. "Nice guys don't invite a woman to a show and forget."

"Could we please talk about something else? Besides, what do you know about being a nice guy, Jude Davenport?" she scoffed, leaning forward, too, and pinning him beneath her blue-green gaze.

Knowing she was one hundred percent focused on him threw Jude. Good grief, her attention was heady.

"More than the guys you hang out with, apparently." He stared right back, liking everything about the way he felt staring into her eyes and that this time she held his gaze, not backing down or looking away even as electricity sparked between them.

Excitement licked his imagination and visions of kissing that full mouth of hers danced through his mind, of placing his palms against those cheeks of hers, staring into her eyes, and kissing her until her taste filled his senses.

Visions of his taking her on that date and giving her the night she should have had and making up for what the idiot had done to her.

"Think whatever you will, Sarah." He even liked saying her name, how it rolled off his tongue almost melodically. "But I can honestly say that if you'd been dressed up for a date with me, I wouldn't have forgotten you no matter what the hell came up."

"That's good to know." Eyes glinting, she pursed her lips.

At her comment, Jude raised his brow, to which her lips parted, tempting him further. His mouth craved hers with a dizzying intensity.

"That's not what I mean," she began, looking flustered. "I mean… Oh, you know what I meant and what I didn't mean."

"Do I?" His lips trembled from unfamiliar restraint at not taking what he wanted. She was so close, yet he knew he shouldn't kiss her, that he had no right to kiss Sarah.

"Oh, get real, Jude. I am not your type and you are certainly not mine. What your dating practices are really don't pertain to me." Even as she protested, he heard the question in her voice and understood why. Normally, he'd have already kissed those disapproving pink lips of hers.

He wanted to kiss them.

Wanted to kiss her.

All of her.

That he hadn't kissed her said something, but he wasn't sure he understood exactly what or why he was so hesitant to make a move.

"Certainly not your type?" he pushed, knowing he wasn't reading her wrong, that, despite whatever she thought of him, there was powerful chemistry burning between them.

"Certainly," she repeated with a slight slur, making him wonder how many glasses of wine she'd had while he'd been finishing their dinner.

"Why is it that I'm certainly not your type, Sarah?"

She blinked, then gave a haughty little tilt to her chin. "Because I'm not into men who sleep with so many different women."

Were they back to that?

"I think you overestimate my prowess."

She broke eye contact and laughed. "Nice try, Casanova."

He watched her toy with her wine. "What type of men are you into?"

Not answering for several moments, she seemed to search for the answer in her glass.

"Ones who aren't like you," she finally said.

Although her response didn't surprise him, he frowned. "That's not an answer."

"Sure it is."

"How so?"

"It means I'm into men who aren't adrenaline junkies, who have steady, stable jobs, who don't feel the need to have the most notches on their bedpost."

Her response gained passion with each word, making him wonder if she was trying to convince him or herself.

"You know, guys who aren't like you." She emphasized the last word.

Was that how she saw him? The same way the rest of the world did, no doubt. Still, her words stung in ways the words of a woman he'd technically only met that day shouldn't sting. They had no relationship, had just lived next to each other since she'd bought the apartment next to his. Thank goodness he'd not bought the place as he'd considered to expand his own again, mainly to widen his view of the city. He'd hate to have gone through life without the pleasure of having met his neighbor.

"None of those things disqualify me," he pointed

out, taking in every nuance of her facial expression. "Because none of those things describe me."

She didn't look convinced at his denial. "You aren't an adrenaline junkie?"

"No."

"Right." She rolled her eyes. "A man who runs into a burning building?"

"I run into burning buildings because there are people inside who need help or when there's a chance of putting out the fire and saving the building from total destruction."

Emotion flickered in her gaze, like the shimmering of the sea. She didn't break eye contact, just narrowed her gaze, as if she fought letting herself believe him. "You don't get a rush out of fighting fires?"

"I didn't say that." He shrugged. "I get a rush when I save someone's life, but not from the actual going into the burning building or risking my own life."

Although doing so did make him feel more alive, more like the man he'd been before Nina had fallen for Charles and then died.

Maybe every time he saved a life he somehow felt vindicated that he'd not been able to save the woman he'd loved, that he'd turned his back on her and their friendship when he couldn't have more. Not that he could have saved Nina. She'd chosen Charles, had died due to childbirth complications. There had been nothing anyone could have done. Had there been, Charles and Jude both would have given their lives for Nina's.

Except when he fought fires, Jude had felt half-dead since the moment he'd cut Nina completely out of his life, lost his best friend, and destroyed the closeness he'd once shared with his cousin.

He didn't feel half-dead now. Quite the opposite.

He didn't recall ever feeling as alive as he felt at this moment, staring into the eyes of a woman who didn't think much of him, but who was as intrigued by him as he was her, despite the fact that she didn't want to be.

Which meant what exactly? He didn't want a relationship, was no longer a relationship kind of guy. These days, he took women to his bed, not to his dining room to feed them a meal he'd cooked.

He sure didn't long to take women on dates where he showered them with romance and attention to make up for every wrong they'd ever endured.

Yet, looking into Sarah's eyes, that was exactly what he wanted. Hell.

"I think I'm more your type than you want to admit, Doc."

As Sarah helped Jude clear the table and load his dishwasher, his words kept running through her head.

Surprisingly, this was the first silence they'd had as they'd chatted away during dinner. Jude was a great conversationalist. He made intelligent comments, listened with eager ears, and responded with insightful observations.

The few dates she'd ever gone on had left her feeling awkward and socially inept. Eventually, she'd almost quit dating, because why bother? She wasn't looking for a man in her life, knew what being involved with the wrong man could cost a woman, and didn't appreciate giving up a night of her life to feel inadequate at the end of the evening.

The few times she'd made exceptions had never ended well.

For instance, the night interesting Kenny Goodall had asked to take her to her first Broadway show. She'd lost the glasses, donned mascara and lipstick, put on a decently fitting dress, and anxiously awaited what had promised to be a wonderful evening.

She'd never felt so mortified, unattractive, and convinced her mother was right in all her life as when she'd discovered he'd forgotten their plans.

Never again would she allow herself to be so humiliated at the hands of a man.

Nothing about her dinner with Jude made her feel inadequate, though. Quite the opposite. She'd enjoyed sharing the meal with him more than she'd have dreamed possible. Maybe because she knew there could never be anything between them.

The fact he'd seemed perturbed she'd written him off as not her type and given him her reasons why surprised her, though. Why would he care?

Sure, she'd felt heat when looking at him and he'd made flirty comments at the hospital and tonight, but the reality was she wasn't Jude Davenport's type.

He hadn't bothered to deny that, had just questioned that he wasn't hers.

Before having seen that different side of him at the hospital and tonight, she'd have said it was because he was so arrogant he assumed he was every woman's type.

If gorgeous, intelligent, witty, and full of testosterone were the criteria, then he was.

Sarah glanced around the kitchen, surprised at how quickly they'd gotten everything cleared. Surprised at how amazingly stocked and spacious his kitchen was. She liked the granite countertops, the workstation island, and the stainless-steel appliances.

What she didn't like was that now there was nothing to occupy her hands, more awkwardness was setting in.

"You want another glass of wine?"

Looking at him in relief, she exclaimed, "Yes!"

He must think her a total slush and she rarely drank. She'd just been grateful for something to do with her hands to ward off her own mental demons. She should leave before the awkwardness and inadequacy set in, reminding that she had nothing in common with him.

He poured her another glass, then one for himself. "Let's sit on the sofa and look out at the city. It's my favorite way to end a stressful day."

So maybe they did have a few things in common. Besides chemistry.

Sarah sat, but couldn't relax to enjoy the view as she had earlier because Jude sat down beside her. His body wasn't touching hers, but he was closer than he should be since they were the only two people on his large sofa.

Why had he sat so close? If she took a deep breath, she'd probably brush up against his arm.

She finished off her glass of wine in record time, set the glass on an end table coaster, and stood. Enough was enough. She'd had a mostly enjoyable night with him and wasn't going to ruin it by staying longer.

"Thank you for the delicious meal, for turning off my smoke detector, and for letting me enjoy your view."

First placing his glass next to hers on the table, he stood, stared down at her. "You are very welcome, Sarah, but I should be thanking you."

The intensity in his blue eyes about had her almost sitting back down because of wobbly legs. "For what?"

"Providing excellent dinner company and turning my night into something memorable."

She hadn't done that. Wasn't going to do that. Was that what he thought she was there to do?

"I'd best be going," she ventured, not breaking eye contact with him but taking a step back.

His eyes twinkled. "In a rush?"

"It's been a long day. I look forward to going to sleep." Yes, she had put emphasis on the word "sleep". "I'm sure you feel the same."

One side of his mouth crooked upward. "Then I guess I have no choice but to say good night."

Sarah barely held back her sigh of relief. Which was just as well, because Jude did the unthinkable.

He kissed her.

Just a short peck on her mouth with his warm lips, but one she felt ricochet all the way to her toes and bring every nerve cell to life along the way. The power of Zeus, she thought again, knowing she'd been struck by lightning.

"Goodnight, Sarah," he said, his lips still so close she could feel his warm breath caress her sensitized mouth. He looked straight into her eyes, his full of what she could only describe as desire.

Desire. For her.

No doubt hers shone the same way.

Because she felt desire. For him.

His lips touched hers again, this time slower, exploring her mouth with his soft, tender touch. He stared into her eyes, searching them as surely as his mouth explored her lips.

She shouldn't be kissing him. He was a scoundrel, a good-for-nothing womanizer who used women.

Only, deep down, he wasn't.

She shouldn't be kissing him. He wasn't her type.

Only, deep down, he was.

She shouldn't be kissing him. She wasn't his type.

Only he was looking at her, kissing her, as if she was.

His kiss was so sweet, so addictive, so electrifying, that she didn't want him to stop.

So she kissed him back.

Kissed him with the same exploration of his lips, his mouth, that he had kissed her with. At some point her hands found their way to his shoulders, to his neck, to his soft dark hair that she now threaded her fingers through, toying with the silky strands.

Never had she experienced a kiss like this.

Never had she felt a man's body like his.

Strong, hard, capable of amazing things, focused completely on her every movement, her every response, her every breath.

She didn't stop him when he cupped her face to kiss her more fully, when his hands worked their way down her shoulders, to her back to settle low and pull her against him.

Oh.

He was long and lean and hard. All man, the kind who rushed into burning buildings to save little girls. The kind who could sweep a woman off her feet without having to catch his breath. The kind whose eyes seduced with just a glimpse.

The kind whose body made a woman want to explore every inch, feel every inch, claim every inch as her own.

That's how she kissed him, not bothering to hold anything back. What was the point? The moment was some anomaly in time that would never happen again. She'd worry about regrets and recriminations later. Much later.

Jude kissed with a passion she found addictive and she gave in to how she craved him.

His hands shifted to her shoulders, and to her

surprise he pulled back, stared into her eyes with ones that appeared as dazed as she felt.

Which was saying a lot. Her legs had all the strength of melted butter. Which was a pretty accurate description of how the rest of her felt, too.

"That was some goodnight kiss, Doc."

She wasn't sure how to take his comment. Was he making fun of how she'd kissed him after claiming he wasn't her type?

"Um, y-yeah, it w-was," she stammered. "Nothing like any I've encountered, for sure."

"Really?"

He seemed intrigued by her comment and Sarah regretted her wine-induced confession. At least, she was blaming her blurting out that she'd never been kissed like that before on the wine.

Honestly, she could just as easily blame it on his kiss because the man's mouth had outright intoxicated her.

Squaring up her shoulders and trying to achieve a look of nonchalance, she nodded. "Don't act like it's a big deal because I'm sure you get that a lot."

"Get what a lot?"

Oh, the things she could respond with, but, even though she should be blaring a reminder over and over in her head, the last thing she wanted to do at the moment was think about him with other women.

"The reaction that you are a way above average kisser."

Looking more than a little pleased at her answer, he chuckled. "Way above average?"

His pleasure in her response, that he was looking at her with affection rather than mockery, freed Sarah of her embarrassment at her confession.

Or maybe it was the wine freeing her of her inhibitions. Yep, she was going to keep blaming the wine. Nasty inhibition-lowering stuff.

"Okay," she admitted with a little roll of her eyes and a smile of her own. "You're phenomenal and make my previous kissing experiences seem like they were conducted by preschoolers."

He stroked his thumb across her cheek. "Preschoolers?"

"They weren't," she assured him, thinking she should quit talking any moment now. "I have been kissed since preschool."

His thumb made a circular caress over her cheekbone and her brain went a little fuzzy for a moment. For a moment? Ha, her brain had been fuzzy all evening. Looking at him made her brain fuzzy. Kissing him had completely fuzzed her.

"I wasn't actually kissed in preschool," she clarified. "Not even once, although this little boy named Johnny chased me around saying he was going to kiss me when he caught me, but I never let him catch me." She should shut up, because why was she telling him about Johnny from preschool? "I have been kissed. By grown men. Good, decent men who were my type."

At least, she'd thought they were her type. Now she wasn't so sure.

"But they didn't kiss like you." Yeah, she really should quit talking.

The color of Jude's eyes deepened, darkening with an emotion Sarah couldn't label. Instinctively, she liked his warm expression, though. She liked it a lot.

"How did I kiss, Sarah?"

He cupped her face now, stared into her eyes, and his voice had a husky tone to it that made her want to listen to him say her name over and over.

All night long.

Wine, stop it.

"Like you could set my body on fire and make me happy to go up in flames."

Oops. That had slipped out. Maybe she needed to zip her lips.

Zip her lips?

She was reverting to preschool.

Or maybe the way Jude was looking at her, touching her, had her intelligence on hold.

He quirked a brow. "You know my job is to put out fires, right?"

"My guess is that you've started more than a few, too." She swallowed, half expecting him to sweep her off her feet and carry her to his bedroom all Rhett Butler style.

Would she stop him?

Or would she give in to the curiosity of how good Jude Davenport could make her feel? Because she knew being the focus of this man's attention in bed would be unlike anything she'd ever imagined possible.

Before that moment, that was, because right now her imagination was endless.

Jude stared into her eyes for long moments. "What are you doing tomorrow evening, Sarah Grayson?"

CHAPTER SIX

CONFUSED, SARAH BLINKED. Tomorrow evening? Shouldn't he be worried about what she was doing right then? At that moment? In the next fifteen minutes? No, Jude wouldn't be a fifteen-minute man. He'd be hours and hours.

There went her imagination again. Endless.

"Working," she answered, thinking he couldn't really have just asked if she was busy, because she didn't expect him to want more than just a rumble between his sheets.

Or was that his normal routine? Make the woman think he was interested in more than just one night before luring her into his bed?

Hadn't he already figured out that she needed no further luring? She was curious and purring for more.

"How about Friday evening?" he asked, his thumb sliding across her cheek. "Are you working then?"

Her forehead scrunched. "No, but—"

"Plans?"

"No, but—" She was going to tell him she didn't want idle promises of seeing him again. If she agreed. And she would. Why not let a man like Jude introduce her to what all the sex hype was about? *Sexual Orgasm for Beginners?*

Ha! She'd bet anything he'd move straight into an advanced course. Maybe *Advanced Multiple Wows*, or something along those lines.

"Would you give me the privilege of taking you to your first Broadway show on Friday evening?"

Their minds clearly on two different subjects, Sarah's head spun and she frowned at him in bewilderment. "Why would you want to do that?"

Why was he talking about Friday evening when they were in the here and now and his bedroom was only a few feet away?

"I'd like to take you to watch *Phantom of the Opera.*"

"What? Why?"

"I'd like to fulfill that desire of yours."

Which was where her brain had been, not on watching a play. But he meant…he was saying… asking…

"As a…" she'd been going to say "friend", but, whatever they were, they weren't friends "…neighbor?"

He chuckled. "As someone who'd like to kiss you goodnight again. Soon."

"Oh." She bit her lower lip. Part of her wanted to throw caution to the wind and say yes, and to please just go ahead and kiss her again right now, like she'd thought he was going to do. Would that be soon enough? But she wasn't a throw-caution-to-the-wind kind of girl. She was a logical girl who avoided men like him because they used women. She knew he used women. She saw the parade of usees leaving his apartment the morning after.

She was not a usee. She'd been thinking about becoming one, had even been thinking of using him to give her the pleasure wielded at his fingertips, which would make her a user, too. What she hadn't been thinking of was going on a date with Jude Davenport.

That terrified her much more than the thought of having sex with him.

Sex was nothing to Jude. Maybe dates weren't either. But to her, at that moment, dragging him into his bedroom and stripping him naked felt safer than agreeing to a date.

No.

She would not set herself up for that particular disappointment again.

"I can tell you are way over-thinking this," he pointed out, lifting her chin to where she was looking into his eyes again. "It's just a date, Sarah."

Just a date. She hadn't misread what he'd been offering. Jude wanted to take her on a date. A real date.

"I'm not your type," she reminded him, positive that agreeing to go with him would be a bad idea, that to do so would be setting herself up for disappointment the way Kenny had never come close to.

What if she grew emotionally attached?

No, she knew better than to do that with a man like Jude. If they went out, it would be because he was tired tonight, but was interested in pursuing the sexual chemistry between them at a later time. On Friday night. Taking her to watch a Broadway show was no big deal to Jude, merely a form of foreplay.

She needed to be careful not to make his offer into more than what it was.

"And I'm not your type," he countered her response, his eyes full of delicious promise. "So how about you say you'll go to dinner and to see *Phantom of the Opera* with me? We will have a good time. I'll be on my best behavior and give you a night you'll never forget. I give my word."

The man could sell sand in the middle of the desert.

"And then what?" she ventured, trying to play out in her mind what would happen after their "date". "You expect me to sleep with you and then me to sneak out of your apartment the next morning?"

His expression didn't waver. "I would never ask you to sneak out of my apartment, Sarah."

Right. He'd just kiss her goodbye, while standing in his doorway with only a towel covering his lean hips, while she craved more of whatever he'd done the night before.

If she wasn't careful, she'd be the one with no pride, offering to do whatever he wanted for just a little bit more of his delicious body.

She had to put a stop to this. Her sexual need had

ebbed a little and she felt stronger, more able to walk away, and that's exactly what she was going to do.

She went to turn from him, but he stopped her.

"I like you, Sarah," he told her, his voice clear, sincere, imploring. "I've enjoyed tonight more than I've enjoyed talking with a woman in a long time. Stop judging me on what you think you know. Pretend you met me for the first time at the hospital today and listen to what your heart is saying right now."

If she'd met him at the hospital and not had preconceived ideas she might think he was wonderful and not at all like the men her mother had warned her about.

"My heart isn't saying anything right now." Okay, so it was beating fast, and a little erratically, but that wasn't speech.

He put his palm over her heart, as if interpreting an unspoken language.

Beating a *lot* erratically, she corrected, wondering why his hand on her chest made breathing so difficult.

"Maybe you just aren't listening closely enough, because I think it is."

"Don't use lines on me, Jude Davenport," she warned, reminding herself not to get caught up in what he was saying. The man was a practiced womanizer. "I'm not one of your women."

Looking frustrated, he sighed. "How about we go to dinner and the show Friday evening and then just have some fun between now and Christmas? You get to decide how much, or how little, happens between us physically."

No doubt shock registered in her eyes because his question floored her. That a lot would happen between them physically wasn't in question. If she spent time with him, she would end up in his bed. She didn't fool herself otherwise. She didn't even deny to herself that a big part of her wanted to be in his bed, to know what it felt like to have him give her body pleasure.

"Christmas?" she finally croaked. "Christmas is weeks away. Wouldn't Thanksgiving make more sense?"

Which almost sounded as if she was considering his outrageous suggestion. She wasn't, was she?

He shrugged. "Why not Christmas? Thanksgiving is only a few weeks from now. We've already admitted that we're dreading the holidays. Why not spend them together so maybe they won't be so bad?"

Sarah mentally shook her head. Jude was asking her to date him through Christmas?

Had she passed out in her kitchen from smoke fumes and only dreamed he'd come to rescue her?

That made more sense.

Reality was that she was unconscious, suffering from smoke intoxication, and having one heck of a hallucination.

Either that, or Jude must have enjoyed their kiss.

She had enjoyed their kiss.

Had truly never been kissed that way, had never felt so much passion bubbling within her.

Yep, she must be hallucinating.

She bit the inside of her lip. Ouch. The pain was real. Which meant this was real. That Jude was searching her eyes, looking for an answer.

The truth was that she wanted to know him better, too.

If she said no, she'd only be denying herself. But there was that thing she didn't really want to think about. Before she could consider agreeing to any of this, she had to address it or else it would be a constant thorn.

"What about the other women?"

"What other women?" He glanced around his living room. "I only see you."

"You know what I mean."

"I'm not that shallow, Sarah."

When she didn't relent, he sighed. "You want me to sign my name in blood that I won't see other women?"

"You can do whatever you want. Whoever you want," she clarified. "Just not on my time. If I agree to this, then I don't want other women in your apartment."

Surprisingly, he didn't tell her she was crazy, that she had no right to make demands. Instead, he regarded her a moment, then asked, "You'll do the same?"

His question was laughable.

"I don't have men come and go out of my apartment."

"You go to their apartments?" he pushed.

"No."

His brow arched. "You do date?"

Not often. Dating wasn't high on her list of

things to do. Never had been. She'd watched too many women squander their lives away chasing after that elusive "the one". Most of the time, she was smarter than that.

At the moment she didn't feel smart. She'd thought Jude wanted to take her to bed and instead he was trying to talk her into agreeing to spend the next several weeks dating him.

A smart woman would have already agreed.

Or was it that a smart woman would have already left his apartment? Or never been there to begin with?

"That guy, the one who stood you up, you have been on a date since that night?"

She winced at the reminder of just how miserable dating gone wrong could make her feel. Instead, she'd cling to how good his kiss had made her feel, to the knowledge that he wanted to kiss her again.

"Occasionally," she answered, trying to stay focused on their conversation rather than all the things running through her mind. "My priorities haven't been on how many notches I could put on my bedpost."

Although she'd been striking out, he didn't seem offended by her comment.

"What have your priorities been?"

"Not on getting laid."

"I think it's safe to say you've established that." His gaze narrowed. "You do think notches are my priority?"

They were talking in circles. She took another step back, determined she was going to make her way to her apartment.

"I don't know you well enough to know your priorities."

"Which I plan to remedy," he countered.

Flustered, she put her hands on her hips and glared. "You seriously want to take me to a Broadway show? To date me, just me, through Christmas?"

Eyes glimmering, he grinned. "Absolutely."

She had to say yes, didn't she? Only a fool would say no to what he was offering. As long as she stayed focused on the facts, that they weren't in a real relationship but a temporary one, that she didn't want a real relationship any more than he did, everything would be fine.

She met his gaze and even before she said a single word, victory shone in his eyes.

"You know if you stand me up I'll put cockroaches under your apartment door," she warned.

Not looking worried, he grinned. "Cockroaches?"

"Or worse."

Rather than say something teasing back, he cupped her cheek. "I won't stand you up, Sarah. But I'm glad to hear that you refuse to let any man, myself included, treat you shabbily." His hold tightened ever so slightly. "Make sure you don't stand me up."

As if.

The emergency room had been busy. Busy enough that Sarah hadn't been able to dwell on her date with Jude the following night.

Not so busy that she hadn't paused outside her apartment to stare at his closed door that morning.

Not so busy that she hadn't answered his text messages saying good morning, then telling her to have a good afternoon, then messaging her that he'd been called in to the station that night but looked forward to seeing her the following evening.

He really planned to take her out.

If he stood her up, she'd be devastated. As much as she hated to admit that truth, she acknowledged it. Wasn't that why she'd never let a man pick her up at her new apartment? Because she didn't want her beloved home tainted by painful memories of being stood up?

Yet she'd agreed to go out with Jude.

Which meant she needed to figure out what she was going to wear.

Typically she dressed to avoid attracting any type of attention from the opposite sex. Doing so had just made life easier through med school and as an emergency room physician. Trying to appear attractive garnered attention she didn't want, hence the thick glasses sitting on her face that weren't prescription but that she wore any time she left her house.

Camouflage? Or self-defense?

While typing up the report on the last patient she'd seen, for a kidney stone, she mentally ran through the items in her closet.

Nothing there suitable for a dinner and show with Jude Davenport.

Unless she wanted to put on the dress she'd worn the night Kenny had been a no-show. Not going to happen.

She wasn't much of a shopper, but she supposed she could search tomorrow to find something. Not on Fifth Avenue, where most of Jude's dates probably shopped, but surely she could find something decent at an upscale department store or second-hand shop?

Maybe she'd even stop by the make-up counter and have her face done while there.

Or maybe she was being ridiculous in considering trying to spiff herself up to impress Jude. If she spiffed non-stop between now and tomorrow evening, she'd never rival the beauties she'd seen leaving his apartment.

Plus, the last time she'd spiffed up had gone horribly wrong and had ended with her looking like a raccoon from the tears she'd cried when she'd called Kenny and realized he'd forgotten he'd asked her out…and was out on a date with someone else. She'd not bothered to tell Jude that part.

Why humiliate herself even further than she already had?

She finished up her notes on the patients she'd cared for during her shift, then logged off the computer system.

"You heading out?" her friend Shelley asked.

Sarah stood, stretching her spine. "Yes. Today wasn't as bad as yesterday, thank goodness, but it's definitely been another long one."

"Speaking of yesterday, how's the little girl? The one rescued by that hunky firefighter who saved her life and made me want to take him home to give him some tender loving care and a good scrub down."

Sarah's cheeks flamed at Shelley's mention of Jude. He'd been the one to give her the tender loving care, along with a delicious meal. No scrub down. They'd both already showered by the time she'd set off her alarm.

"Keeley's good," she said, thinking of the little girl she'd checked on several times throughout her shift. She'd even gotten permission from Keeley's mother to text Jude to let him know about the child. "She recovered consciousness this evening.

Hopefully, she'll be weaned off the vent before the night is through."

Sarah spoke with her friend a few more minutes, considered mentioning that she had a date with the hunky firefighter, but decided not to. They hadn't actually gone on a date so she shouldn't jump the gun, just in case.

Not that she thought Jude would stand her up. With her history, she should be terrified he would change his mind, that he'd find some excuse to cancel their date. There was a tiny part of her that acknowledged the possibility, but her gut instinct was that he wouldn't do that. Something about him exuded honor and integrity.

Which was ridiculous when she knew he was a scoundrel when it came to women.

But if she didn't live next door to him, if she hadn't seen the plethora of women parading in and out of his apartment, if they really had met yesterday at the hospital, she'd have thought him a really great guy. A hero kind of guy.

Which might be testament to how foolish she was being over the man.

She was still thinking about Jude when she said hi to their apartment building doorman, while she rode the elevator up to their floor, when she stepped out of the elevator and made her way down the corridor. She'd not taken but a few steps when she noticed the large, brightly wrapped box with a huge gold bow propped against her apartment door.

A present?

She didn't have to wonder from who, because there could only be one person who'd do such a thing.

CHAPTER SEVEN

SARAH DIDN'T WANT to be excited, but was as she
bent and pulled the card with her name on it off
the box.

Heart pounding, goofy smile tugging at her
mouth, reminding herself not to read too much into
anything Jude did, she ripped into the envelope.

*I planned to give you this in person, but got
called to the fire hall. Can't wait to see you in
this tomorrow night. Wear your hair up and
forget your glasses so I can see your lovely
face.*

Her heart muscles squeezed a little too tight at
his last line. Because of the past, she told herself.

Besides, if the man had bought her underwear
she was going to place the order for cockroaches.

Not really. She'd put whatever skimpy piece of
silk and lace the box held on and model for him.

She'd probably be wearing a goofy smile to go with it, too.

But even if the size of the box hadn't already suggested otherwise, when she picked up the box, she knew whatever was inside was more than underwear.

Feeling like a kid in anticipation of Christmas morning and trying to remind herself there wasn't really a Santa Claus and she shouldn't be so keyed up, she unlocked her door, stepped inside, stripped off her winter layers, then carried the box to her coffee table.

Rather than open it, she sat on her sofa and stared at the package as if it might contain a rattlesnake.

Or the cure to cancer.

She was both eagerly excited to see what the box held but also afraid of what gift he might have given.

Or maybe it was a consolation prize because he planned to cancel after all?

No, he'd said he couldn't wait to see her in it and, truly, she couldn't see him doing that, not with how passionate he'd been about Kenny having done so.

Taking care, she pulled the ribbon off from

around the box, then lifted the lid, and moved aside the tissue paper.

Oh, my.

Inside were a small gold-foil-covered box, a shoe-sized box, and the most beautiful dress she'd ever seen.

Had she gone shopping she never could have found anything so perfect in color and style.

Not that the items were likely to fit right. Not with her lack of curves, and how would Jude have known her size? But the sea-green dress was gorgeous, modestly cut, and very close to the color of her eyes.

She ran her finger over the silky material. Not too flashy, not too revealing, yet definitely something more figure-flattering than she'd ever worn. What size was it?

She moved the material aside to where she could see the label. Oh, wow. She dropped the material for fear she might damage the dress. She might be a fashion wreck, but even she recognized the designer and that the dress would have had a hefty price tag.

Christmas morning excitement or not, she couldn't wear the dress. She didn't want Jude spending money on her. That wasn't who she was. As a matter of fact, she'd planned to offer to pay for her show ticket and dinner.

Not that she'd thought he'd let her, but she would have been sincere in her offer to do so.

With shaky hands she picked up the shoe box, knowing what she'd find inside, and lifted the lid. Matching designer shoes in her exact size with medium-height heels. Smart man in choosing a pair that wouldn't make her feet hurt or make her walk like a shaky newborn fawn.

Again, the designer name on the shoe was one she recognized, but not one she'd ever splurged to purchase.

Unless he'd seen her size in the shoes she'd slipped off her feet while snuggled up on his sofa, drinking her wine, she had no clue how he'd known what size to buy. Good grief, the man paid attention to details.

A dress, shoes…she could only guess what was in the small box. The skimpy panties she'd imagined earlier?

She was wrong. Very wrong.

Inside was a velvet jewelry case.

If she'd thought her hands had been shaky before, now they shook with full-blown tremors. Earthquake-sized ones that probably had some Richter-scale-watching scientist freaking out as he tried to track down the source.

Holding her breath, she flipped open the box lid.

Inside was a stunning pair of dangling, sparkling earrings that surely to goodness weren't real diamonds, and a folded piece of paper with a handwritten message.

I won't forget.

Her eyes watered. He wouldn't. He'd be there. He'd bought her a dress, shoes, and earrings to wear. She'd never been given clothes or jewelry by a man. Not ever.

The only jewelry she owned was a gold chain with a quote pendant on it that her mother had given her at her high school graduation and that she rarely took off.

To thine own self be true

She pulled the chain from beneath the layers of her scrubs and long-sleeved undershirt and fingered the charm.

She wasn't quite sure how to take Jude's gifts.

Obviously, from his luxurious apartment, he didn't live on a firefighter's pay but on the deep Davenport dollars. He probably had trust funds. The gifts meant nothing to him, but were likely commonplace things he did for women.

If so, no wonder they came to him in droves.

What was she saying? If he gave them no gift except his time and body, women would come to Jude in droves.

She would come to him.

She didn't want gifts. She wanted…him.

She closed her watery eyes, took a deep breath, then pulled out her phone to text him a "thank you, but not necessary" note. She'd barely hit send when her phone rang with his number showing on the screen.

"Sorry I wasn't there to give them to you in person. I'd like to have watched you open them," he said by way of greeting. "Tell me you were smiling."

"I was smiling," she admitted. "They are lovely, Jude, but I have clothes and if I needed new ones I can afford to go shopping." Not on the scale of what he'd sent her, but she did make a decent living. "Like I said in my text, buying me gifts wasn't necessary."

Unless he had wanted her dressed a certain way, up to a certain social standard in case they ran into friends? She couldn't convince herself of that from a man who hung out in a fire hall, who hadn't cared who'd seen him dirty and smelly at the hospital. He didn't come across as a social snob, but she supposed anything was possible.

"I didn't think it necessary," he countered over the phone. "I wanted to give them to you."

Sarah fought sucking in a deep breath.

"I want tomorrow night, my taking you to your first Broadway show, to be everything you ever dreamed, to make up for the last time you thought you were going."

She bit the inside of her lower lip and squeezed the phone a little tighter in hope of steadying her hand. "You don't need to make up for another man's wrongs, Jude."

Which was the first time she'd ever admitted out loud that Kenny had done something wrong. Even to him, she'd accepted his explanation that he'd forgotten, made other plans, but that she understood, right? Because he and Sarah were just going as friends anyway, right?

"No," Jude agreed. "But I want to."

She closed her eyes, told her heartbeat to slow down before it pounded out of her chest. "You always do what you want?"

"Not always."

"Most of the time?"

"Yes."

Did that mean he hadn't wanted to have sex with her the night before? She'd thought...no, she'd known that's what he'd wanted. He'd just been tired. She'd been tired. He'd promised he wouldn't trick her into his bed if she came to dinner and he'd kept his promise.

Not that he would have had to trick her. All he'd had to do was crook his finger and she'd have followed wherever he led.

Just like Brandy. Ugh.

"Should I remind you that I'm not like the women you usually date?" She definitely needed to remind herself of the women he usually dated.

"No reason to. I already know you're not like the women I usually date."

She'd swear she could hear amusement in his

voice, but what he found funny, she wasn't sure. Regardless, his light-hearted tone eased some of her tension. Some, but not all.

"You giving expensive gifts makes me uncomfortable."

"You shouldn't be uncomfortable, Sarah," he assured her in a more serious voice. "I don't want you to think the gifts came with strings attached. They didn't. I gave them to you because I wanted you to have them, because giving them to you gave me pleasure, and my only regret is that I wasn't there to watch your face while you opened them."

She wasn't sure she believed him. She had no reason to. Then again, she had no reason not to other than her mother's voice blaring through her head.

"Okay," she ventured, leaning back on the sofa and staring at her presents. "Thank you. They are lovely."

"So are you. Did the dress fit?"

He thought she was lovely? Good grief, why was a man's compliments and excitement flabbergasting her so? She was logical, reasonable, too smart to be swayed by pretty words.

"I don't know," she admitted, swayed by his

pretty words because she was smiling that goofy smile again and no matter how she tried to wipe it off her face, she couldn't. So much for logic and reason. "I haven't tried it on."

"What?" He sounded truly surprised. "I thought you would have done so first thing."

"I just walked in the door from work," she reminded him, pulling off her shoes and tucking her feet up under her on the sofa.

"Busy day?"

"I work in the emergency department at Manhattan Mercy. Every day is a busy day."

"Touché."

"Speaking of which, are you related to my boss?" She'd almost asked Charles today, but hadn't wanted to risk his asking why she wanted to know. She could have just said she lived next door to Jude, but she'd been afraid Charles might see things she didn't want seen.

There was a moment of silence, then Jude said, "He's my cousin."

Jude hadn't asked who she meant, which meant he'd already made the connection. Of course he had. He'd seen her at the hospital where his family was practically royalty.

"I thought you must be related. Your eye color is so similar to his. You should have told me. Might have helped your cause to mention your relationship to Charles. I'd be hard-pressed to name a man I admire more."

There was another brief silence, then, rather than take advantage of the opening she'd given him, he ignored her compliments about his cousin and said, "Try on your dress, Sarah."

She frowned at her phone.

"Why are you changing the subject? I adore Charles. If I had family of the caliber of Charles Davenport I'd make sure the whole world knew we were related."

"Yeah, well, when you're a Davenport the whole world tends to know a lot about you, whether you want them to or not." His voice had lost its happy edge and had taken on a dark one.

Apparently, Jude did not want to discuss his family with her. Fine. So they weren't that kind of dating. Not the kind that shared about their family and met each other's families and were invited to family functions.

Well, that was good to know. Helped her keep things in perspective.

Not that she wasn't planning to do that already. She knew they were only temporary.

"I'm not going to try on my dress until after I've taken a shower." Maybe because she had hospital grime on her. Maybe because she was feeling contrary. "And then, I still might not tonight."

Her bets were leaning toward the latter.

"If you don't then I'll question if you're female."

The teasing tone she was used to was back and a tightness inside her unwound.

"I'm definitely female. Been that way my whole life," she assured him, glad that the dark edge had left his voice as quickly as it had appeared. "But whether the dress fits or not really isn't relevant, because even if it's a perfect fit, I'm not sure I'll wear it. It's not my usual style."

The dress was a perfect fit and Sarah was wearing it.

At the moment.

She'd contemplated changing a dozen times. Every time she'd walked to her closet and tried to come up with something else to wear to her Broadway show date, she'd not seen anything to tempt her to change.

Instead her gaze would fall on the black dress she'd worn the last time she'd planned to go to see *Phantom of the Opera* and an uneasy feeling would twist her gut.

Maybe she should have spent the day shopping.

Instead, she'd done laundry, cleaned her apartment, bought groceries. All the things she typically did on her day off even when she didn't have a date with her hunky neighbor.

Her very handsome neighbor whom she'd not seen since he'd kissed her goodnight two nights ago.

What if he saw her and was disappointed?

What if she'd been wrong and he didn't show?

Her nervousness was just foolishness, wasn't it?

No, it wasn't. He wasn't going to stand her up. No matter how many ghosts from the past haunted her mind, she refused to let them take hold. Her nervousness stemmed from so much more than fear of rejection and humiliation.

Her fears came from what would happen after their date.

Jude might have said he didn't expect anything in return, but a man didn't bother sending a woman a dress, shoes, and jewelry unless he wanted something.

She knew what he wanted. It was what they both wanted. Her question was why? He didn't have to do gifts to get women into his bed, to get her into his bed. If anything, his gifts made her that much more skeptical. Was he toying with her? Seeing her as a challenge?

A make-over challenge?

Wouldn't he be in for a surprise? Although she had on the dress he'd sent, the shoes that were surprisingly comfortable or she'd not have kept them on fifteen seconds, and the sparkly earrings, she'd not done anything more than brush a little mascara across her lashes and gloss on some lip balm to prevent chapping.

She glanced down at her glasses sitting on the bathroom sink counter. She didn't need them to see, but she had a feeling she'd need them in other ways before the night ended. She slid them onto her face and instantly felt calmer.

She had this. She was in control. Not Jude. What happened tonight was up to her. Even he'd said so.

When she opened her apartment door and he

stood there, in a tux, holding flowers, she wasn't so sure about that control.

He looked like the hero straight from a romantic movie. Only she was no fun, quirky heroine. She was…just her.

A just her that felt prickles in her eyes. Prickles she fought because she was not going to end up with raccoon eyes tonight.

"You are beautiful."

She went to deny his claim and chide him for his use of lines again, then realized he was sincere. He looked at her with true appreciation, with true admiration in his blue eyes. So she just stared at him in a bit of awe, blushed, and murmured thanks.

"I was wrong about wanting you to put up your hair. I like it better loose the way you have it. I'd never seen you with your hair down or I'd have suggested it to begin with. It's gorgeous."

Ha. She'd left it loose because she had felt contrary about being a yes girl who did everything he said and she hadn't wanted her neck exposed. At least, she'd thought she didn't want that. Maybe she did.

He didn't comment on her glasses, but she knew he'd noted that she'd put them on despite his knowing she didn't need them and that he'd asked her not to.

She wasn't sure why, but in her mind contrariness to being a yes girl equaled control of what was happening between them. Or as close as she was going to manage.

"Do you have a coat?"

"I'm not going out there like this. I'd freeze," she countered, then realized how brusque and rude she sounded. She needed to just embrace the wonderfulness of what he was doing for her and forget contrariness. "Sorry. I'm a bit on edge."

"I'd never let you freeze." His eyes had that twinkle that told he'd come up with all sorts of interesting ways to keep her warm. "I don't want you tense, Sarah. This is supposed to be a fun night for you."

"It's impossible for me not to be on edge when I don't understand why you're doing this," she admitted, pushing her glasses up a little on the bridge of her nose.

He watched her movement, grinned. "Doing what?"

"Taking me on a date."

"You are a beautiful, intelligent woman who I

had a great time with a couple of nights ago and who I want to get to know better." He leaned forward and dropped a kiss on her forehead. "Smile, Sarah. You have no reason to be nervous of me. My priority is for you to have the best night of your life."

Sarah sucked in a deep breath. She couldn't help it. She was positive that at no point in her life had anyone wanted to give her that. Not her mother. Not anyone.

"That's a good priority."

"Isn't it, though?" He brushed a long strand of hair away from her face, and smiled a smile that made her heart skip a beat. "Grab your coat and let's head out. The car is waiting."

Expecting to see a taxi, Sarah's feet froze in her new heels when she caught sight of the long black stretch limo pulled up to the curb in front of the building.

Taking in his proud smile, she choked, "What have you done?"

His pleasure at her reaction was as obvious as the huge smile on his face. "Arranged a ride to the theater."

"A taxi would have done just fine."

He squeezed her hand. "Tonight's not a taxi kind of night."

She cut her gaze to him. "Why not?"

He lifted her gloved hand to his lips and pressed a kiss there. "I promised the best night of your life, remember?"

"Mission accomplished."

His smile widened. "Good."

"I know I've said it before, but I'll say it again. All this isn't necessary."

"All this is very necessary," he assured. "Tonight is a night of firsts."

He had no idea.

Or maybe he did. Maybe that was why he was going to the extra trouble. Although if he was really the womanizer she'd initially labeled him as she supposed it didn't make sense that he'd go to so much trouble.

"Your first Broadway show," he clarified, grinning, and his eyes sparkling with mischief. "Our first date."

"Probably our last," she added, with an eye roll because she was scared if she kept looking at him he might see just how touched she was by how much effort he'd gone to.

"Such an optimist," he teased, and tucked her hand between his. "You agreed to through Christmas. I'm holding you to that. Don't you expect to enjoy yourself?"

She did expect to enjoy tonight. Very much. Like a fairy-tale princess on her way to the ball with the handsome prince. A heroic prince who fought fire-breathing dragons and carried her away in his chariot.

"Also my first limo ride," she said, offering him a small smile.

When her gaze connected with his, what she saw there stole her breath. So did his next words.

"Then I'm even happier I didn't go for a taxi."

The driver opened the passenger door and held out his hand to assist her. Sarah climbed into the car, slid across the seat to make room for Jude.

Make room for him? Half their apartment complex could fit inside the thing.

"The driver will take us to the Majestic and pick us up afterward. We have reservations for dinner at—" he named a French restaurant she'd heard of, but had never been to "—and then afterward I have a surprise I think you'll enjoy."

Sarah wasn't really a surprise kind of girl. There

had been too many unknowns during her childhood for that. None of them ever good. She liked having a plan and knowing what to expect so she could prepare.

Besides, afterward? The show would last a few hours, then dinner. That would put them well past ten, probably close to eleven. Just what did he have planned? Maybe he really was some type of superman, but she needed sleep.

She wasn't scheduled in the emergency room the next day, but she did have things she planned to do.

She glanced around the inside of the limo, at the pure luxuriousness of the interior, then over at the man sitting beside her.

Looking like an eager kid to give her whatever his surprise was, he grinned and her heart jerked.

Careful, Sarah. Not only is Jude exactly what your mother has warned you about your whole life, he's got more layers than you'd have ever given him credit for.

Because the man sitting beside her looked completely comfortable in his tuxedo. Completely and utterly breathtaking, too.

No more so than he'd been in his jeans and T-shirt the other night.

Or in his towel.

Or even in his dirty uniform.

She might even prefer the dirty uniform look because it had been one she could relate to, one that had cracked through the preconceived ideas she'd had about him.

A look that made him real, human, vulnerable.

Vulnerable?

Ha! The man sitting next to her looked about as vulnerable as a double zero agent from a British spy flick.

"This is the quietest you've been since we've met."

"That's not true. I didn't say a single word on the morning you were telling Brandy goodbye."

Why did the memory of him kissing the woman sting so deeply? Why did she always revert to throwing other women between them?

Because she needed something to keep her from forgetting none of this was real, that she didn't want it to be real.

CHAPTER EIGHT

"That morning doesn't count."

At his comment, Sarah glanced toward Jude.

"You and I hadn't met," he clarified. "I didn't even know your name, despite the fact that I had said hi to you a couple of times."

He had. Sarah had ignored him, pretending not to hear, or had just mumbled a reply without looking his way.

Why was that? She wasn't a rude person, wasn't unfriendly. She'd made friends with other tenants in the building. But for some reason she'd felt the need to keep a safe distance from Jude.

Because he was a womanizing playboy.

Only she couldn't say he'd been anything other than a gentleman to her. At the hospital. When he'd rescued her from her screaming alarm. When he'd cooked dinner for her and shared his magnificent view of the city.

When he'd kissed her goodnight.

When he'd surprised her with presents, shown up at her door with flowers, arranged for a limousine for their date, and promised the best night of her life.

He'd been pretty close to perfect since they'd met, which made him about as unsafe as was possible.

Unable to stop herself, she faced him, stared at his mouth. She didn't question whether or not he'd kiss her tonight. He would.

He wouldn't push or force himself upon her. He'd be just as he had been the other night. He'd give her control as to how far they went and seemed to have no issue with relinquishing that power to her.

She was in control of what happened between them.

Her.

As long as she remembered that, held onto that control, she was fine.

"Can I?"

"Can you what?" she asked, wondering if she'd been so lost in her thoughts that she'd missed his having said something.

"Kiss you."

The man's powers of observation were quite terrifying.

"It wouldn't be a goodnight kiss."

His lips turned up a little at one corner. "I guess that depends on your definition of a good night."

Because he planned to give her a good night.

And not kiss her goodnight, but good morning, instead. She could see it in his eyes.

And feel it to her very core.

He was wining and dining her so she'd be agreeable.

Which she already was.

So instead of answering his question, she turned to look out the window. "I love the city, you know. Not just the skyline, but the people, too. Where else in the world can you see so many people from different walks of life within just a few blocks?"

"Not many."

"There's nowhere else like Manhattan," she defended the city she adored.

"True. Have you visited many places, Sarah?"

Heat rushed into her face again. He must think her such an uncultured bumpkin compared to the social circles he traveled in as a Davenport.

"Not many," she admitted. She had barely left

Manhattan. There was no need. She loved every-thing about where she lived.

"Your favorite place?" Apparently, realizing what she was about to say, he added, "Besides the obvious."

"London," she answered, although she'd never been. Had never even flown. It was just a place she'd thought she'd like to visit someday. A city whose heartbeat reminded her of her own beloved New York's. "Look." She gestured out the limo's window. "We're about to see Times Square."

His grin was infectious. "You're one of those who stand out there every New Year's Eve to watch the ball drop, aren't you?"

"Absolutely, and don't you dare laugh at me." It was something she'd done for as long as she could recall. She and her mother would stand in the crowded throng of happy partygoers and cheer in the New Year, thinking January was going to bring good things into their lives. Those hopeful moments were some of Sarah's best memories.

The one time her mother was optimistic rather than full of negativity.

"So no worries that you'll turn into a pumpkin at the midnight hour?"

Her lips twitched. "Not on New Year's Eve, at any rate."

The driver pulled the limo to the curb and came around to open their door.

Sarah's breath caught. She was at the Majestic. To watch a real, live Broadway show. One she'd fantasized about for years.

Another throwback to her mother, no doubt, as she recalled them watching the film over and over while Sarah had been growing up.

Now she was going to watch the show live, had arrived in style with a gorgeous man.

Maybe she really had suffered smoke inhalation from her burnt toast and was still locked away in some fantasy world where men like Jude Davenport showered attention on women like her.

If so, she'd enjoy every moment of her delirium.

Excitement burned through her veins and, as she took Jude's outstretched hand and stepped out of the limo, she smiled. A real smile. One that filled all of her being and left no room for anything other than pure joy.

"Thank you."

"For?" Jude almost stumbled backward. Not because of the people moving around him but because of the woman radiating inner beauty toward him.

Sarah was breathtaking.

How he'd not noticed that months ago was mind-boggling, but now that he had, he wanted to soak in her exquisiteness.

Just as he wanted to see that smile over and over and was apparently willing to go to great lengths to do so.

Which made him question why he was going to such lengths with Sarah. Possibly the hurt he'd seen in her eyes over the idiot who'd stood her up and Jude wanting to erase that pain, to replace those memories with ones so magical she'd never doubt her value again. That she'd never let any man dump on her, because she'd not seen herself as worthy of better. He'd show her how she deserved to be treated so in the future she'd not settle for some man who didn't appreciate what a treasure she was.

Not that Jude liked to think of her with another man, but he wasn't a relationship kind of guy. He'd been a fool to think he had been with Nina. He'd learned better and that wasn't a lesson he'd forget.

Keeping Sarah's hand tucked in his, he guided

them through the crowd and into the line to enter the theater.

"This. Thank you. Thank you. Thank you." She glanced around, taking in the ornate decorations visible through the open doors. "This is so beautiful."

Her excitement was contagious and Jude couldn't keep the smile off his face. Everything about Sarah was delightful. Any moment he expected her to spin around as if she were in a dream. Good. That's how he wanted her to feel.

"Just wait until you are inside the actual theater."

Excited blue-green eyes met his. "That good, huh?"

He hadn't necessarily thought about it being so on his previous visit, but he knew seeing the theater, the production, through Sarah's eyes was going to be an entirely different experience for him.

That everything, through Sarah's eyes, was new.

"That good," he agreed, pulling their tickets out of his jacket's inside pocket.

They made their way to their seats and he was glad they were as good as the sales agent had promised. He wanted tonight to be as amazing as Sarah had dreamed of. Better.

Her face shone with the excitement of someone who had looked forward to this moment for a long time and he was the lucky guy who got to share it with her.

Why hadn't she gone on her own when it was something she'd wanted to do for years? Why hadn't she gone with a friend? With a family member? By herself?

"Look. There's the chandelier!"

He chuckled. "Shh, you're supposed to be pretending that you don't see that yet."

She laughed and ran her gaze over the ornate ceiling. "I can't believe I'm here. I'm really here."

At one point in the show, she grabbed his hand and, not seeming to notice, held on.

Jude didn't mind. He enjoyed Sarah's warm, capable hand holding his.

A hand that could save a life.

A hand that could pull him closer or push him away.

No doubt before everything was said and done she'd do both.

A heaviness settled over his chest.

Sarah was different from any woman he'd known. He'd recognized that immediately, had been intrigued by her outside his apartment door, impressed by her at the hospital, fascinated by her at her apartment, protective of her at his, enthralled by her tonight.

There had been few times in his life when he'd made an effort to impress a woman.

Nina. He'd tried to impress her. And he had. As her friend. They'd been great friends, the best, had had lots in common, but Charles was who she'd given her heart to. Wonderful, perfect, brilliant Charles.

He wondered a moment if he was crazy when he began comparing the past with the present, when he wondered if there was something dark inside him that had caused Nina to fall for Charles instead. Jude had wanted to love her, to give her the world, and protect her. She'd loved his cousin and Jude hadn't been able to forgive her for that, not even when it had cost him her friendship and undermined his relationship with his family.

Since then, he'd not dated anyone, just had a flurry of one-night stands that had meant nothing more than physical satisfaction and reminders he didn't have to be alone but chose to be.

He glanced at Sarah, his mind racing in a thousand directions as he watched the play of expressions behind her ridiculous glasses.

Perhaps sensing he was looking at her, she squeezed his hand, her gaze glued to the lavishly dressed cast on the stage. "This is amazing," she whispered.

She was right. This was amazing, but he didn't mean the production.

He lifted her hand to his lips and pressed a kiss there, momentarily distracting her from the show.

She blinked at him. "What was that for?"

"For coming with me tonight."

"I should be the one kissing you for inviting me tonight."

Wanting his melancholy thoughts gone, he waggled his brows. "I'd be okay with that."

Smiling, she rolled her eyes. "I bet you would."

The stage caught her attention again and Jude forced his attention back there, too. Not that his focus lasted more than a few seconds. Because to his surprise Sarah leaned over and pressed a kiss to his cheek, then went back to watching the show as if nothing had happened.

Something had happened.

Something intense and deep and as swirling with rich emotion as the show.

Sarah had kissed him and he'd swear whatever that dark something inside him was, her sweet kiss had just cracked it wide open.

Sarah doubted Jude would accuse her of being quiet again that night. From the moment the show had ended and they'd gotten back into the limo, she'd been talking non-stop.

With an amused look on his face, he let her chat away, which was just as well because she didn't think she'd have been able to hold back her excitement if she'd had to.

"I thought my heart was going to stop when..." She elaborated on one of the scenes.

"I noticed tears rolling down your cheeks in that part," he pointed out, his smile indulgent.

"My glasses were supposed to keep you from noticing things like that."

His brow rose. "Is that what they were for?"

She knew what he meant and she wasn't going there. "That and the things glasses are usually for."

"Have you forgotten that I know you don't need those things to see?"

"I haven't forgotten."

"But felt the need to wear them tonight to shield yourself from whatever it is you don't want me to see?"

Something like that, she admitted to herself. They were part of the armor she'd been wearing for years.

"I think you see plenty despite the fact I have my glasses on," she accused.

"You hungry?" he asked, surprising her by his subject change.

"Starved," she confessed, telling the truth. "I didn't eat much earlier. I was nervous about tonight."

"Your nerves have settled now?"

"Now my nerves are so electrified from that amazing show that everything else pales in comparison," she gushed, not caring he probably thought she was silly for being so excited. "I have such a rush from the show I'm surprised I even notice I'm hungry."

He laughed and the sound reverberated through her chest and mind, setting off happy bells.

"Just you wait," he promised. "The best is yet to come."

"No food is going to compare to what we just witnessed."

"I take it back," Sarah recanted an hour later as her lips closed around her spoon. The most delightful sugary concoction melted in her mouth and sent pleasure through her from head to toe. "Pretty sure this stuff is straight from heaven."

"Like it?"

Rather than answer him, she took another bite and slowly withdrew her spoon from her mouth. "I'm positive it's illegal and some type of mind-altering goodness that makes the whole world seem absolutely euphoric."

He chuckled. "I assure you it's perfectly legal."

"I know," she admitted, meeting his gaze. "I didn't mean to imply you'd drug me. I don't think that at all."

"I never thought that's what you meant." His eyes twinkled. "Neither would I ever do that to you."

"You wouldn't have to.

Her admission had Jude swallowing hard and her mouth watering. Not because of the dessert.

He'd been the perfect date. Kind, thoughtful, generous, attentive, sweet.

"I've enjoyed myself tonight, Sarah."

"You make it sound as if you don't usually enjoy yourself and we both know better than that," she reminded him, as much for herself as him. She might not do this kind of thing often—ever—but Jude did.

"You're referring to sex. I'm not."

She didn't bother to hide her disbelief. "You're saying sex isn't enjoyable?"

"Sex is extremely enjoyable," he clarified. "That's why it's so popular. But I was referring to a different kind of enjoying myself."

Her heart pounded, the beat echoing through her head. "Does that mean we're friends?"

"No, Sarah, I don't think that's what that means."

"I'm confused." She took another pleasurable bite, trying not to let the fact that he'd stopped eating altogether and was just watching her do so bother her.

"No need for confusion. I meant I enjoyed your company in ways that have nothing to do with sex."

She wasn't sure whether to be insulted or complimented. What was she thinking? Wasn't she the girl who always claimed to want to be appreciated for her mind? For her personality? For what was inside rather than her physical appearance? For her brain rather than her body? Wasn't that why she downplayed her physical appearance to keep from attracting the wrong kind of attention?

The wrong kind? She hadn't attracted any attention in a long time. Not that she'd been trying. She hadn't. The opposite, actually, because she didn't want a relationship.

Her efforts had worked. No one had noticed her. Not her brain or her personality or anything about her.

Not until Jude.

He'd noticed her buried beneath her coat, scarf, and hat. The memory of how his eyes had glinted when he'd looked at hers that morning assured that.

He'd immediately recognized her at the hospital. *Sans* hat, coat, and scarf, even.

Sure, he had seen her in the apartment hallway a few times, but he'd never looked at her prior to that morning, and when he had looked, he'd noticed.

Despite all the reasons he shouldn't have—like that she'd been hidden beneath a dozen, figurative and literal, layers and that he'd been with another woman.

"You're a complicated man, Jude."

He laughed. "Me? Complicated? I'm the least complicated Davenport you'll ever meet."

She shook her head. "That's not true. You have so many aspects to how you really are you make my head spin."

That was why she felt a little dizzy when looking at him, thinking of him. There couldn't be any other reason.

"What you see is what you get," he pointed out, as if that somehow made his claim true.

She knew better.

"Every time I see you, I see something different."

That seemed to intrigue him. "In what way?"

"For instance, right now, you are the very opposite from the man who stayed at the hospital with Keeley."

With a look of disappointment, he shook his head in denial. "I'm exactly the same man who stayed with Keeley. What's 'very opposite' is what's on the outside."

"Explain," she said, hoping he would because she knew his doing so would give her insight he rarely revealed.

"What you see on the outside tonight is what you lump into being a Davenport. That's not who I am."

"You're not a Davenport?"

"By blood, yes, but I'm not like my family."

"In what ways?" Because she'd swear he was a lot like her boss. A good man, only Jude was a whole lot sexier than his handsome cousin could ever hope to be.

"I don't fit in with them, Sarah. Neither do I want to."

"More of a 'march to the beat of your own drum' kind of man?"

He shrugged. "I suppose. From an early age, I knew I wasn't going to grow up to make the family proud."

Which sounded odd to Sarah because he was a man who risked his life on a regular basis. Surely that he was so heroic made his family proud?

"Tell me about growing up as a Davenport," she

said, because she wanted to know everything there was about him, to understand why he didn't think he belonged in his prestigious family.

He shrugged. "Not much to tell that you couldn't read in the papers or assume about the kid of a wealthy family. I went to all the right schools, did all the socially expected things of the wealthy, and was fairly miserable."

"A poor little rich kid kind of thing?"

He snorted. "I guess. But don't feel sorry for me. My parents loved me. Still do. They're just waiting on me to get my wild ways out of my system and take my right place within the family."

"Which is?"

"Not being a firefighter."

"Is that why you do it?"

He shook his head. "Not even on days when I'm most frustrated with my family."

"How did you end up running into buildings on fire? I doubt you just woke up one day and realized that's what you were meant to do in life."

"When I was fifteen I lived at the private school I was attending. One of the kids in my dormitory decided to give smoking a try late one night and ended up setting the building on fire. The place was old, couldn't have met fire codes, and went up in flames."

"Oh, no! Was anyone hurt?"

He shook his head. "Because of where the fire had started, everyone on my floor was trapped. Even now I remember the terror of my classmates, and how, when the fire department rescued us, I was fascinated by those who risked their lives to save others. From that point on, much to my family's disappointment, fighting fires is the only profession I can imagine making me happy."

She took his hand and squeezed it. "For whatever it's worth, I'm very proud of you and what you do, Jude."

He didn't say anything, just stared at her in a way that made her feel as if he were trying to see inside her head.

Trying not to be overly self-conscious at the intensity of his stare, she finished her dessert.

After he'd paid for their lavish meal and their coats had been brought to them, Sarah was still fighting self-consciousness.

"Don't do it," Jude said from beside her.

"What?" she asked, letting him help her into her coat.

"Whatever it is you're thinking."

She turned, met his gaze, and felt her tension ease at the sincerity she saw there. Goodness, he was unlike anyone she'd ever known. In a good way.

She arched her brow and gave him what she hoped was a flirty look. "Fine. I won't, but it's your loss."

He gave a wry grin. "Because you were going to throw yourself at me in the foyer of an exclusive French restaurant?"

Pretending shock, she covered her mouth with her fingertips. "How did you know?"

His eyes darkened and he took her hand into his. "You win," he conceded, pressing his lips to the top of her hand, as he continued in a tone that was only half teasing. "I take it back. Do it. Please, just do it."

The fact his words tempted her to do exactly that, that his lips were soft, warm, electrifying against her fingertips, should probably worry her. But at the moment she just felt glorious and as if she was the envy of every woman who'd seen them that night, as if she were floating through some amazing fantasy that was too good to be true.

"Too late," she teased. "The moment is lost for-ever." But as she stared into his sparkly blue eyes, she mentally corrected herself.

This moment was forever.

CHAPTER NINE

JUDE MIGHT BE in over his head.

Way over his head.

He'd never told anyone, not even Nina, about how he'd felt about his family, about why he'd become a firefighter. Why had he opened up to Sarah?

He'd not even thought about it, just answered when she'd asked, as if what he was saying was no big deal.

What was it about Sarah that made telling her things easy? As if spilling his guts to her was the most natural thing in the world?

That she hadn't judged him, hadn't found him lacking for not embracing what it meant to be a Davenport, surprised him. He was used to women who were with him as much due to the Davenport name as they were for him.

Not that there weren't advantages to being born wealthy and a part of the Davenport clan.

For instance, Sarah's surprise.

Penny, his daredevil cousin, had been over the moon at his request. Then again, she'd have likely agreed just to meet Sarah.

He'd made the mistake of mentioning a name, of mentioning how much Sarah loved the city, of how he wanted to show New York to her in a way she'd never seen it.

What better way than from Penny's helicopter?

Or so he'd thought until that moment.

Sarah's face had gone a ghastly pale shade at the sight of the helicopter.

"We're going somewhere in that?" she asked, her voice strained.

"You're not afraid of flying, are you?" He'd not considered that possibility, but knew there were lots of people who didn't fly.

"No." Her tone didn't sound confident. "At least, I don't think I am. I don't know." She gave him a trembling smile and shrugged. "I've never been in a helicopter."

Protectiveness swept over him. An odd protectiveness that felt different from any he'd ever experienced until she'd been telling him about her failed date. Just as then, he wanted to take on her fear, her doubt, and give her the world.

He gave her hand a reassuring squeeze.

"You'll like this," he assured her, hoping he was correct. "Penny is a great pilot. You'll like her."

Still eyeing the helicopter, she asked, "Penny?"

"My cousin Penny," he clarified. "She said she knew you. Among other things, she's a paramedic with Manhattan Mercy's air ambulance."

"Penny Davenport. Your cousin. Charles's younger sister. Of course." She glanced at him and a new uncertainty crept into her eyes. "You get along with her, then?"

He nodded. "She's crazy, like me."

"You don't care if she knows you're with me?"

Not what he'd been expecting Sarah to ask, neither did he understand why she had.

He frowned. "Why would I care if she knows?"

Insecurity shone behind her glasses. "I… I just wondered. I wasn't sure how much your family knew about your women."

Maybe because he was concerned he'd miscalculated on the helicopter trip or maybe in retaliation for the vulnerability he felt at the intense protectiveness she evoked in him, Sarah's comment made him angry. Enough was enough.

"You're not one of my women, Sarah."

She wasn't. She was…hurt by his outburst.

He could see it in how she averted her gaze, in how she looked even more tentatively at the helicopter, in how her grip on his hand loosened.

"That didn't come out right," he began, wanting to rake his fingers through his hair but knowing Penny was watching from where she now stood next to the helicopter. "Let's not talk about other women, Sarah. They don't matter." They never had, but especially they didn't at that moment, when he was looking into Sarah's eyes and wanting to recapture the magic that had sparkled there when they'd left the theater, when they'd been at the restaurant, before he'd spilt his guts to her. "Okay?"

"Fine by me." But there was no sparkle as she eyed the helicopter, just wariness.

"Sarah?" His pretty cousin with long, wavy chocolate-brown hair greeted them. Her eyes were the same blue as Jude's, that piercing Davenport blue that his family was famous for and that they couldn't escape.

"I know we've bumped into each other in the emergency department from time to time," Penny continued. "But we've never officially met. It's nice to meet you."

Sarah went to shake the woman's hand, but got pulled into a hug instead.

Seconds later, Penny had him in a death-grip hug, too. To be so tiny, his cousin packed a punch. He'd always connected to Penny on a level he hadn't with the rest of his family. Maybe because they were both risk-takers and didn't fall into line with family expectations.

"It's good to know my cousin's taste is improving," Penny teased, giving him a playful punch in the shoulder, much as one of his male friends might do.

Sarah's gaze cut to him, as if assessing how she was supposed to respond to Penny's comment since they'd just agreed not to discuss other women.

"As if yours is any better," he teased his cousin back, determined he was going to recapture the joy from earlier. "You ready for this?"

"Absolutely." Penny turned excited eyes toward Sarah. "I'd have sworn Jude didn't have a romantic bone in his body. I was so impressed by his call there was no way I could say no."

Sarah's feet shifted. Jude doubted it was because of her new shoes. "Romantic?"

"Quit giving away my surprise, cuz."

Smiling, Penny rushed them into the helicopter, gave them a quick safety rundown, headsets to put on, and then they were off.

Sarah's hand gripped his for dear life. He glanced at her and questioned himself again. Maybe he should have saved the helicopter for another night.

"Open your eyes, Sarah."

"No." She shook her head back and forth in tiny little movements. The rest of her body was stiff, as if she was afraid to move for fear she might trigger a tailspin that would send them crashing to the ground. "I can't."

Her hand had become clammy against his and Jude mentally swore.

"Have you ever flown in any type of aircraft, Sarah?"

She shook her head.

"Another first, eh?"

Which he probably should not have said as Penny's gaze briefly cut toward them.

"My stomach is still on the ground." Her face was pale, her hand clammy, her lower lip half-hidden between her teeth.

Then she trembled.

Aw, hell. Jude's stomach dropped to the ground, too, because there went that crazy, strange protectiveness again.

So he did what he had to do.

He pressed his lips to Sarah's.

Her eyes sprang open and her teeth freed her swollen lower lip.

Eyes locked with hers, he continued to kiss her, to taste her, to caress her mouth with his. Slowly, she relaxed, her grip on his hand taking on new purpose.

"Hi," he whispered against her lips when they finally separated a few millimeters.

Gaze locked with his, full of trust and so much more, she smiled the sweetest smile he'd ever seen. "Hi back."

His insides flooded with emotion, he searched her eyes. "You okay?"

"I am now."

"Good answer." He leaned his forehead against hers, the top of her glasses pressing against his face as he stared into her eyes. "I can have Penny take us back."

Sarah shook her head. "I think I'm okay now."

Brave girl.

"But you're missing your surprise."

To which she turned to look out the helicopter. "Wow."

In a few seconds, she relaxed further, but still held onto his hand with a bit of death grip as she stared out at what he'd wanted her to see.

What he'd wanted to share with her.

The New York City skyline from the air.

Penny flew them over the bay, along acceptable flight routes, lingered at all the right places, as if she could somehow hear Sarah's breath catch over the loud buzz of the helicopter.

When they arrived back at the helicopter pad, Sarah gushed her thanks to Penny, who waved off the praise, hugged Sarah again, and gave Jude an approving thumbs-up that caused heat in his cheeks that some might have called a blush, but he knew better.

Within minutes, Jude and Sarah were back in the limo on their way home.

Home.

To his home.

Or her home.

Or to each their own?

As she leaned her head against his shoulder, squeezed his arm and thanked him for the most amazing night of her life, he knew the answer.

Sarah grew more and more antsy as the elevator made its way to their floor. Did she invite Jude into her apartment? Was that how this worked?

Or would he invite her into his?

Either way, she wanted what this night would bring. She couldn't imagine any better conclusion to their wonderful evening than to spend the night in bed with Jude.

That would be the grand finale.

The real surprise.

The first of all firsts.

What would make her stomach soar and drop in ways Penny's helicopter never could.

Feeling self-conscious, she reached out and took his hand, startling him in the process.

He'd been lost in thought for most of the limo ride home. Which had been okay by her, because she'd rested up against him and felt an inner peace at where they were.

Did she have any expectations of Jude beyond the night?

No. She knew better. She didn't even expect him to stay interested until Christmas. She was just another in a long line of women to enjoy the wonderful man he was.

Which didn't exactly thrill her, but he hadn't made any pretense of anything else. Other than that he'd said they'd enjoy each other through Christmas.

Which was so much more than she'd had to distract her from the holiday blah just a few days ago.

She walked beside him down the hallway, planning to take his lead on whether to invite him to her place or to eagerly follow him into his.

He stopped outside her apartment, so she dug into her coat pocket and pulled out her key.

Fumbling a little, she unlocked the door, but didn't turn the handle, just looked up at him. "Are you coming inside with me, Jude?"

He closed his eyes. "Do you want me to come inside with you, Sarah?"

"What do you think?"

"That I want you to come with me tomorrow evening to a party at my station."

Stunned, Sarah blinked. "A party at your fire station?"

He nodded. "The crew will be cleaned up and have their partners with them. It's an annual pre-Thanksgiving meal, of sorts. I'd like you to go with me."

"But…won't they wonder who I am?"

A V formed on his forehead. "Why would they? I'll introduce you. They're a rowdy bunch, but I wouldn't trade them for any other."

He was inviting her to go with him to a party at his fire hall. To introduce her to his coworkers. He was letting her know tonight wasn't a one-night stand, that there would be a tomorrow night.

Smiling, she nodded. "I'd love to go with you, Jude."

"Great." He let out a sigh of relief, then bent and kissed her with the quickest of pecks on her eagerly waiting lips. "I'll text you the exact details in the morning and pick you up about seven tomorrow evening. We'll take a taxi if that's okay with you?"

Did he think he'd set a precedent with the limo that he'd have to constantly repeat?

"I usually walk most places I go," she reminded him, not wanting him to confuse her with someone who expected grand gestures all the time. "We can do that, or take a taxi if walking to your station is too far."

"It's not that far, but we'll take a taxi." With that he took a step back from her and didn't quite meet her eyes as he said, "See you tomorrow, Doc."

With that he opened her apartment door, practically picked her up and set her inside, handed her keys to her, then pulled the door closed.

With him on the other side.

Jude leaned against Sarah's door and fought the urge to rip it off to get back to her.

What had he just done? Turned down an offer from a woman he wanted more than he'd ever wanted any other?

He'd lost his mind. Had to have.

But going into her apartment with her, knowing what would happen, wouldn't have been right.

Not with Sarah.

Not when spending the night with her would

make her think she was no different from any other woman he'd ever known.

She was. So very different.

He wasn't playing for keeps so what she thought shouldn't matter so much, but it did.

She wasn't one of his women.

He wouldn't, couldn't, treat her as if she was.

CHAPTER TEN

ALTHOUGH SARAH HAD other plans, she spent the day at a mall instead. Not her favorite thing to do any time of year but as the holiday season was getting under way, the crowds made the whole outing that much more intimidating.

She was intimidated.

She bought clothes to hide her body, to blend in with her surroundings, to not be noticed, things she ordered online and didn't care if they hung on her body all wrong.

That wasn't going to work today.

She wanted to be noticed as a woman.

She didn't want to blend into the background and be a faceless, shapeless, asexual person.

She wanted Jude to notice her.

Correction, she wanted Jude to want her. To want her in every way a man could want a woman.

Which seemed a silly thought. He did want her. She'd seen desire in his eyes repeatedly throughout the evening before. She wasn't blind. Desire had been there and real. What she didn't understand was why he'd shoved her inside her apartment and high-tailed it.

Her towel-wearing, bedroom revolving door wielding neighbor had not taken what she'd wanted to give him.

Had he thought she'd follow him out of her apartment, to perhaps beg for more, as Brandy had?

Wrong. She'd wanted to spend the night with him, but was not pathetic. She had her pride, her morals. She would not cling or beg. Ever.

She didn't want to have to beg.

Funny, she believed one hundred percent that had she been willing on the night he'd cooked her dinner he'd have taken her to his bed. Last night she had been, and he'd sent her to bed alone. What had changed?

The man really was complicated.

Had he not asked her to go with him tonight she might have questioned whether or not he'd been as attracted as she'd thought, if he'd really enjoyed himself. He'd seemed to, smiling, flirting, charming her hesitations away, but what did she know of such things?

Not much. Too little experience.

Now she wanted to seduce him, to be irresistible to him. Was that even possible?

Ugh. Her head hurt from just considering all the things that had happened between now and the morning when she'd stepped out of her apartment and found a towel-and-woman-wrapped Jude.

"Quit squinting your eyes," the sales clerk ordered, stepping back to survey her work. She turned Sarah first one way in the swivel chair and then the other. "That is so much better. Girl, I'd kill for those eyes. And those cheekbones. Are they implants?"

Sarah blinked at the woman whose name tag read "Cher". "What?"

"Your cheekbones." She studied Sarah's face. "Are they fake?"

Fake cheekbones?

"Um, no, they're all mine."

Had Sarah chosen implants, they sure wouldn't have been the cheekbones she had. She'd always thought them too prominent. Besides, if she ever got implants, she had other, mostly flat, areas that could use curves more than her face.

"Lucky you, girl."

"Thank you," Sarah answered automatically, reminding herself the woman complimented customers for a living.

"What color is your dress so I know how to do your eye make-up?"

"I don't know," Sarah admitted. "I ended up in the make-up department before I made it to dresses. I'm going there next to find something."

Cher's eyes widened. "No dress? Girl, we've got to get your dress before I do your eyes. What's your budget?"

Sarah told her what she planned to spend.

The clerk laughed. "You're funny. Leave this to me. My roommate is a personal shopper in Women's. I'll give her a call and she'll fix you right up."

Sarah started to protest then recalled how much she disliked fighting the crowds. "I guess that would work, but make sure she knows I…" She what? Wanted something that would blow Jude's mind, but that still left a lot to the imagination because Sarah wasn't used to skin showing and didn't want to feel self-conscious in front of Jude's coworkers? Did such a dress exist?

The dress Jude had given her for the evening before had been beautiful, had covered up her body, yet had gently hinted at what was beneath. She'd felt feminine without feeling like she was hanging everything out. He'd done a great job. Maybe she should have hired him to buy a dress for tonight.

Only she couldn't afford the name brands he'd sent.

"Something nice, but not too revealing," she told the clerk, who was patiently waiting for Sarah to finish the comment she'd started making. "It's for a date at a fire department party. I've never met any of them except my date and it's only our second date." Or was it third? Did the night she'd set off her smoke detector count? "I don't want to feel as if I'm pulling up my top and tugging down my skirt all night. I will feel out of place as it is, so anything I can do to raise my comfort level is a plus."

Cher smiled and waved away Sarah's concerns. "Like I said, leave this to me. You want sexy without looking as if you're trying. My friend can do subtly sexy. No problem. You'll be the belle of the fire ball and make your firefighter want to take you for a spin on his truck."

Taking out her cellphone and punching in a number, she walked away from a blushing Sarah and began talking. Sarah couldn't make out her exact words but imagined they consisted of things like plain Jane, boring, out of her league.

Not that the clerk knew Sarah was out of her league.

Not once had Sarah told anyone who she was going out with, or even that she was going out at all. Part of her still couldn't fathom why Jude had asked her out, much less asked her a second time to attend a party at his fire hall.

Maybe he wanted someone more normal to take to where he worked than someone a Davenport would typically date. Someone who'd fit in with ordinary people who didn't sing, act, model, or been born into wealth or prestige.

At least that theory made sense, because his wanting to date her for real seemed too far-fetched.

"Wow!" Jude gushed when Sarah opened her apartment door. "I should have sprung for the limo."

Lowering her lashes, layered with mascara, Sarah bit the inside of her painted bottom lip. "Is it too much? You didn't say what I should wear."

Eyeing her like she was the sweetest piece of candy, he shook his head. "It's perfect. You're perfect."

"You don't think I have on too much make-up?" she asked, still not feeling comfortable with the creams and powders Cher had brushed onto her face.

Subtly sexy, that's what Cher had said, promising she was going for a natural, but gorgeous look. Sarah had stared at the finished product in the mirror for a long time, wavering between surprised pleasure and uncertainty at what stared back.

"You are beautiful without the first speck of make-up," Jude assured her. "Tonight you are absolutely stunning."

With the way he was looking at her, she couldn't doubt him. He looked stunned in the best possible way.

Sarah smiled. "Thank you."

"Thank you." He took her hand, spun her around, and whistled. "I'll be the envy of every man there."

That he was verbalizing her thoughts from the night before made Sarah smile.

"Doubtful, but thank you."

They chatted during the short taxi ride over to the fire hall. He paid the driver, and they went into the fire hall. Small groups of friendly people of all sizes and shapes milled around.

"Hey, Davenport!" someone called when they stepped inside the large open area where normally their trucks would be parked, rather than just outside the building.

Jude greeted the man and his wife, then introduced Sarah. "This is my girlfriend, Sarah Grayson."

Sarah couldn't hide her surprise. His girlfriend? Was that what she was? Not just a date, but his girlfriend?

She owed Cher big time.

"Nice to meet you." The man grabbed her hand. "We always suspected this one was holding out on us."

"Oh?" Sarah asked, smiling at the man as she shook his hand, then his wife's. "Does Jude not usually bring someone to these things?"

Shaking his head, the man looked at his wife for confirmation and she said, "Never."

The woman's answer surprised Sarah and she glanced toward Jude, who looked as if he'd rather not be the topic of conversation.

"We were hoping the calendar would help him out. Guess it did."

Expression terse, Jude made a slashing motion, trying to silence the man.

Curiosity piqued, Sarah arched a brow. "The calendar?"

"You don't know?" The man slapped Jude on the back. "Hey, fellas, Davenport didn't tell his girl about his modeling debut."

Jude winced.

"What kind of modeling?" she asked the older man, who was all too eager to tell her.

"Here," another said, coming over to join them. "We'll show you."

"Let's not," Jude interjected, sounding flustered.

"Oh, let's," another added, laughing and joining in as the first flipped the pages of a calendar. "Check out Mr. December."

Jude did something Sarah had never seen him do. He blushed.

Which made it difficult to look away from him to what the men were shoving in front of her. When she glanced down her eyes bulged at what she saw.

Jude Davenport in his fire uniform pants, boots, helmet, and suspenders, but no shirt.

She'd seen him shirtless.

That week.

She knew he boasted a major six pack.

But seeing the visual reminder in print stole her breath. There was nothing subtle about Jude. He was sexy. Seriously sexy.

Knowing his friends were waiting for a response from her, she glanced up and made a scolding noise with her tongue. "Now, honey, you know January is my favorite month, it being the beginning of a new year and all. December is so…commercialized."

Looking relieved at her teasing, Jude shrugged. "December was all they'd give me."

She flipped the calendar pages and let out a low wolf whistle when she got to January. "This guy from the Bronx fire department beat you out?" She gave a disappointed shake of her head, enjoying the men's good-hearted laughter around her.

"Clearly, you are way hotter than him. He must have paid off someone."

"Clearly." He leaned forward and pressed a quick kiss to her lips.

"You must have this one hoodwinked, Davenport," the man who'd brought the calendar over accused with a big grin.

"Nah, she's a smart one. A doctor."

Sarah tried not to beam under Jude's praise, but she puffed out a little at the pride she heard in his voice.

"I think I feel sick," a male voice said from somewhere in the crowd. "I need some mouth to mouth."

Wow. Sarah needed to go back to the mall and give Cher a bigger tip than the generous one she'd slipped into the girl's hand. Obviously, she'd performed miracles.

Subtly sexy.

Sarah would take it.

"Ha, ha." Jude greeted the man, grabbing hands and leaning in toward him in what Sarah called a "bro shake". "Sarah, I'd like you to meet my best friend. Roger, this is Sarah Grayson."

Sarah smiled at the handsome African American man standing next to Jude. "Nice to meet you."

Roger looked her over from top to bottom. Not in a sexual way, more a checking her out to see if she measured up to what his best friend deserved. He must have approved, because his face split with a big smile and he pulled her to him for a hug. "The pleasure is all mine."

"Quit hitting on my girl," Jude warned in a stern voice.

"If you aren't man enough to keep your woman, then it's your own fault if I steal her. Always wanted to date a doctor."

They verbally sparred back and forth a little, all in fun, then Sarah was grabbed by a couple of wives and girlfriends who pulled her over to where several more were uncovering food.

"It's about time he found himself a nice girl to bring with him. And did I hear right? A doctor?"

Cheeks warm, Sarah nodded. "Is there anything I can do to help?" Obviously, the party was pot-luck. "I'm sorry I didn't know to bring something. Jude failed to mention that."

Then again, after her burnt toast it was possible he had purposely not mentioned the party was potluck for fear she'd burn down their apartment building.

The older woman waved her hand in a dismissive motion. "Jude does too much as it is. You just enjoy yourself and that sweet man tonight."

Jude did too much?

"Jude sent food?"

The woman nodded and motioned to where beverages were set up and the huge stack of canned and bottled drinks behind the drink table. "He has all that sent every year. And every year there's always enough to last everyone for their Christmas party and halfway into the new year."

Sarah wasn't crazy about sodas or sport drinks, but she supposed a bunch of people hanging out at a fire hall went through quite a few. Jude's generosity probably saved the crew a pretty penny.

"Plus, he springs for the turkey and ham, has it delivered," another added.

"And he always caters the fire hall Christmas party. He's a good man," one of the women praised.

"I think so," Sarah automatically replied, then realized what she'd said and that she'd meant her words.

Despite her thoughts to the contrary just a few days previously, she did think Jude was a good man.

She glanced toward him, realized he was looking at her, and just to throw him off kilter as much as he threw her off kilter, she winked.

His grin won out on the off-kilter causing, though, because her knees wobbled at how he was looking at her.

"You're a lucky woman."

Sarah turned to the young blonde woman who'd spoken from behind her.

"I'm Cassidy, Roger's on again, off again girlfriend." She smiled and held out her hand. "Currently on again."

Okay. She smiled at the woman. For the next thirty minutes, Sarah talked with the women while the guys did their thing across the room. Every time she glanced Jude's way, he was either looking at her or quickly did, as if he sensed her gaze. Or couldn't go long between looks.

They shared smiles and winks. Sarah was surprised at how comfortable she felt at the party with the group of women. Then again, they were a friendly bunch and all had wonderful things to say about Jude, praising him for his generosity, which apparently extended way beyond what he did at the holiday parties as one commented on how he'd saved him from losing his home when he'd fallen behind due to his wife's medical expenses. Another commented on how Jude had saved the day when he volunteered at every community outreach event. Another went on and on about he'd started a scholarship program for kids of the NYFD.

His crew and their significant others couldn't say enough good things about him. Sarah took their praise in, marveling at just how deep Jude ran.

When the chief called their attention to say grace, Jude made his way over to Sarah, took her hand into his as they bowed their heads.

For the rest of the night he was by her side. Not once did Sarah feel out of place or awkward.

She felt like she was right where she should be. With Jude.

Her mother's voice rang in her head, warning she was being taken in, but Sarah ignored the warning. Her mother had never known a man of the caliber of Jude, not by far. As long as Sarah kept in mind that neither she nor Jude wanted a long-term commitment, everything would be fine.

For the second night in a row, Jude kissed her goodnight outside her apartment door, shoved her inside, and shut the door with him on the other side.

It took her all of thirty seconds to come to terms with the fact that he'd done nothing more than kiss her goodnight again. If that's what you could call it when she snapped out of her shock and flung her door open.

To do what she wasn't sure had he been out in the hallway still.

He wasn't.

He had gone inside his apartment.

For the briefest moment she considered beating on his door, demanding he let her in.

Didn't he know she was subtly sexy tonight for a reason? For him?

Instead, she stared at his closed door a moment, then went back into her apartment, confused that she was the only woman Jude didn't seem willing to sleep with despite her attempt at being irresistible. Go figure.

He hadn't bothered to make plans to see her again.

But she knew he would, that they would see each other again, because they weren't through with each other.

Far, far from it.

CHAPTER ELEVEN

WAS JUDE WORKING? Sarah wondered for the hundredth time that day. Or was he at home? Or doing whatever it was he did on his days off from the fire department? Probably do-gooder things like helping the needy and starting scholarship programs for public servants or—

"Dr. Grayson, the CT results are back on the abdominal pain in Trauma Six," Shelley said, pulling Sarah's thoughts back to the here and now.

"Thanks. I'll be right there." She finished charting despite her distraction, then clicked open the CT results.

Gallstones. Which was consistent with the man's right upper quadrant pain radiating to his shoulder blade, nausea, vomiting, and significantly elevated liver enzymes.

The rest of her shift passed in a busy blur. She didn't have time to pull out her phone to check her messages until right before leaving the hospital.

Excitement hit when she saw the message from Jude. Did she want to have dinner with him at his place?

Yes. Yes, she did.

At his place. Tonight must be the night.

Only it wasn't.

Oh, she had an amazing time with him. First, she'd shared the wonderful meal he'd prepared. Then, snuggled up next to him on his sofa looking out at the city they loved, she'd told him a little about her childhood, about her determination to excel, and the academic scholarships that had funded much of her education.

But when their sofa kisses had heated up to the point Sarah had wanted to rip off his shirt and get up close and personal with Mr. December, he'd pulled back. Quickly thereafter, he'd walked her to her apartment on the grounds they both had to work the following day.

As if that had ever slowed him down in the past.

The next night was similar, almost to the point Sarah found it humorous when she found herself yet again alone on the inside of her apartment door.

* * *

The next night Jude questioned his will power when Sarah decided to take matters into her own hands.

Literally.

They were kissing hot and heavy on his sofa and Sarah wanted more. Lots more.

"Sarah." He attempted to pull back when she fumbled with the snap of his jeans. "Do you like cheesecake?"

"What?" She blinked at him as if he'd lost his mind.

He had.

"Do you like cheesecake?"

"Is that a trick question? Some secret code for an amazing sexual act you want to introduce me to?"

Jude fought groaning. He wanted to introduce Sarah to amazing sexual acts. Lots of them. Not doing so was getting more difficult, but the timing wasn't right.

He wasn't sure what exactly it was that wasn't right, but they should wait longer before having sex.

"I bought dessert but forgot until just now," he blurted out, sensing her frustration. She wasn't the only one frustrated. He was tired of cold showers, but would be taking a murderously long one again tonight. "I wasn't sure which topping you preferred so I got strawberry, blueberry, and cherry."

She frowned. "Are you for real?"

"Last time I checked. Why don't we try some of each topping and see which is best?"

When he started to stand, Sarah grabbed his arm. "Am I doing something wrong?"

She was doing everything right. Too right.

Rather than stand, he leaned back, swept his fingers through his hair, then shook his head. "You couldn't be further from the truth."

"I'm confused."

He felt confused, too, so it only made sense that she'd feel that way. She deserved an explanation. Maybe he could give one without muddling up things.

"I want to take things slow with you," he began.

Her brows formed the V of a deep frown. "Because I'm slow?"

He shook his head. "Because you're different."

She took a few moments before asking, "Is that a bad thing?"

He faced her, clasped her hand with his. "It feels

as if it's a good thing, a very good thing that's worth taking our time and not rushing sex. Don't you agree?"

Gaze locked with his, she squeezed his hand. "You don't have to go slow with me, Jude."

"You're wrong. I need to take things slow."

He couldn't explain it to himself so he sure couldn't explain it to her, but he had to take things slow with Sarah. How much longer he'd have to wait, he wasn't sure, just that sex too soon would ruin things with her.

He'd ruined his relationship with Nina. The circumstances were different, but he wouldn't risk doing the same with Sarah. When this was all said and done, she'd look back on their relationship with a smile, would know she'd been special, would still be his friend.

Anything else was unthinkable.

The following week passed quickly. The emergency department had been crazily busy and Sarah doubted it would slow until after the holidays.

She never knew what would be in the next bay. She'd even taken care of a person who'd been trapped in a collapsed subway. She and Jude spent their evenings together, sometimes late into the night, but he always said goodnight at her door.

Her sexual frustration grew every time she saw him, kissed him, ran her fingers over his strong shoulders.

Sunbeams of happiness sprang to life inside Sarah that he wanted to take things slow with her, but that didn't mean she wasn't above trying to speed him up.

She worked a long shift on Thanksgiving, getting home much later than planned. Jude texted to come over to his place when she had showered after her shift.

She wasn't sure how he'd had time to prepare the scrumptious meal, but was appreciative of the traditional food he served. It had been years since she'd had turkey and dressing on the holidays. She'd gotten her non-existent cooking skills from her mother, unfortunately.

Her mother. She'd called her earlier that day, but had had to leave a message, which hadn't surprised Sarah. Her mother stayed busy with her women's home.

"You're quiet," Jude accused.

Not wanting to talk about her mother, she said the first thing that popped into her head.

"Everyone at the hospital was talking about the photo of Charles and Grace in the paper. Did you see it?"

Not meeting her gaze, Jude fiddled with his fork and didn't answer.

"Apparently they're an item," she continued. "Did you know?"

"No, neither do I care to talk about it."

Sara frowned. "Sorry, I didn't know discussion of family was off limits."

He sighed. "I'd rather hear about your day."

"I was telling you about my day, that everyone was talking about how happy Charles looked in that photo. I had to sneak a peek at break and I agree. I've never seen him so happy."

Why did Sarah want to talk about Charles so much? Not that she knew the reasons why Jude didn't want to think of his cousin, but she seemed to bring him up way too often.

"That's good."

Sarah stared at him, an odd expression on her face. "You don't sound as if it's good."

He shrugged and picked up his plate. "My cousin was seen with a woman. I'm not sure how that warrants his being the topic of our Thanksgiving dinner conversation."

"It's obvious you haven't seen the photo."

Neither did he want to.

"Are you going Black Friday shopping tomorrow?" he asked, to change the subject away from Charles.

"You couldn't pay me to fight those crowds."

"You'll be home tomorrow?"

She nodded. "I plan to sit home all day, catch up on my favorite shows, and veg out."

"Sounds like a relaxing way to spend a day."

"Want to join me?" She gave him a hopeful look. "There's room for two on my sofa."

He'd promised to help Roger move furniture. His friend had said they could do that anytime over the weekend, but they'd agreed on the following day.

"How about I take you to dinner tomorrow evening?"

"I'd like that." She didn't hesitate to agree.

"And Saturday evening? Do you have plans?"

She shook her head. "Hoping to spend as much time as possible with you."

Her words spread warmth through him. Sarah didn't play games, just said what she was thinking. Most of the time he liked that quality.

He liked a lot about the woman he spent most every free moment with. Roger had commented on how much time he was spending with Sarah.

Enough time that he'd gotten to know the woman behind the glasses, the glasses she'd not worn around him all week. She still wore them at the hospital, but she wasn't hiding behind them with him. Not any more.

Which was quite telling.

"How about we stay in and I give you a cooking lesson?"

Her eyes widened with amused surprise. "You want to teach me to cook?"

"Somebody needs to," he teased, loving the light in her sea blue-green eyes.

"Okay, but I should warn you that I make a mean burnt toast and hummus."

"You know, lately I've been craving burnt toast."

Several nights later, Jude made plans for him and Sarah to visit Times Square. He'd noted how she'd gone on when they'd driven past it on the evening he'd taken her to *Phantom of the Opera*. Taking her there felt like the natural thing to do.

Watching her felt natural, too.

Excitement glittering in her eyes, she took a deep breath of the cold November air. "The lights, the people, the sounds, it's magical here. Like inside a snow globe."

He snapped his fingers with feigned remembrance.

"I forgot to arrange the snow," he teased, thinking everything with Sarah was exciting, new, magical. Like inside a snow globe. "Next time I'll remember."

"Ha." Her lips curved in a big smile that twisted his insides. "You know what I mean," she continued. "I know you do. I see it in your eyes when we're sitting on your sofa, staring out at the city. There's a life pulse to this city that is intoxicating."

"That might be the fumes."

"You aren't going to deter me from my appreciation of New York." She shook her hat-covered head. "No way."

"I wouldn't want to." He kissed the tip of her nose, grateful she'd quit hiding behind her ugly glasses.

Still smiling, she glanced around Duffy Square. "Where are we going?"

"To the top of that hotel." He pointed to one of the large skyscrapers facing Times Square.

"I bet the view is amazing."

"Have you been?"

She shook her head. "I've heard the restaurant at the top spins so you have a three-sixty view of the city."

"You heard correctly."

Her eyes shone with excitement. "That is so cool."

He chuckled. "You're easily impressed."

"You think? I've always considered myself picky."

"You're here with me," he reminded her, holding her gloved hand within his as they went inside the hotel and headed to the elevator bank that would take them to the restaurant.

"Exactly."

When he glanced her way, she was smiling like a kid at Christmas. Warmth spread all the way through him.

"You're good for my ego."

She cut her eyes upward. "As if your ego needs stroking."

"It has been a while."

To which she turned to him with wide, accusatory eyes. "Whose fault is that? Not mine, because I'm willing. You're the one who's moving at a tortoise pace."

He laughed and bent to kiss her forehead. "It's going to be all the sweeter when we do, Sarah."

"For the record, sweet isn't the adjective I want to use to describe sex. Make a note of it."

The feeling inside Jude went from warm to inferno. "What adjective do you prefer?"

"Hot? Carnal? Sweaty? Needy? Intense? Desperate?"

Jude groaned at the images her words incited. "You make me want to forget our reservation."

Her eyes burned. "Nothing says we can't."

"Except that I want to show you the city."

"City Schmitty," she mouthed, drawing his gaze to her lips. "Seen one skyline you've seen them all."

Jude smiled, reminding himself he would have this woman, those lips on his body, his lips on her body.

Sarah's tune changed as they ate their dinner in the revolving restaurant. She gushed over the view and talked a mile a minute as she often did in true New York style.

"I do love a good view," she praised. "And it's a good thing I'm cooking again tomorrow evening because otherwise I'm not going to fit into my new clothes."

Jude sat back and listened, thinking she had a long way to go before she wouldn't fit into her clothes, but he appreciated the thought of her not wearing any.

Sex would change everything. If they'd had sex early on, Sarah wouldn't have known the real him, wouldn't have recognized that she was special. Neither would she have believed him if he'd tried to tell her.

There had been too many women. None of them mattered. All had been a means to an end that hadn't worked. Because none of them had changed the past or filled the hole in his chest. None of them had been Nina.

He took the bite of dessert Sarah offered and was struck with a truth. He didn't want Sarah to be Nina.

He wanted her to be Sarah.

Which stunned him a little. A lot.

He didn't need to go slow. Not anymore. Sarah knew him. The real Jude. The flawed Davenport firefighter. She liked him. Wanted him. Was smiling at him as if he was the center of her world.

Only her smile had twisted into a frown and she eyed him suspiciously. "Jude? Are you paying attention to me?"

Staring into her eyes with a clarity he hadn't felt in years, he said, "Absolutely."

Not convinced, she challenged, "What did I just say?"

"That you want to go home and make love to me and use lots of vivid adjectives to describe the experience when I've finished having you all the ways I've dreamed of."

Her jaw dropped. "I didn't say that."

He leaned across the table, stared into her lovely eyes, and arched his brow. "Didn't you?"

"I…" Her eyes darkened to a tumultuous sea color and, without letting her gaze break from his, she nodded. "You're right. That's exactly what I said."

"There's no going back, Sarah. You're sure this is what you want? That I'm who you want?"

He knew the answer. Deep in his gut he knew, but he wanted to hear her say the words.

"Positive." She stood from the table and motioned to their waiter. "Check, please."

Jude hailed a taxi and they rode in silence.

Sarah's brain told her she should feel awkward or nervous, but all she felt was excitement. So much so she couldn't look at Jude because she knew the moment she did she was going to gobble him up.

Literally, figuratively, emotionally, and every way.

So she kept quiet during the taxi ride, during the elevator ride to their floor, and when they stood outside their apartment doors.

"My place or yours?" he asked.

She wasn't sure it mattered, but she immediately answered, "Mine."

He nodded as if he'd known that's what she'd been going to say.

She unlocked her door. They stepped inside. Sarah turned to Jude.

Not to ask him if he wanted a drink.

Not to take his coat.

Not to make polite conversation.

She turned to show him she wanted him, to lead him to her bedroom, and perhaps to keep him there forever.

Jude was way ahead of her.

The second she faced him, he pulled her to him, kissed her lips, her face, pushed her scarf away so he could trail kisses along her throat.

"I want you, Sarah."

"Good." She wanted him to want her. She wanted him to need her. The way she needed him.

Matching him kiss for kiss, she fumbled to get his overcoat off, managed to get the material loose and off him to where it fell to the floor. Her coat quickly followed, as did her hat and gloves.

Grateful for the skin-to-skin contact, she touched him, cradled his face as she kissed him, savored the taste of him, realized how very hungry she was. Starved.

Starved for something she hadn't even known she needed until she'd kissed him.

She tugged at his shirt. "Show me those December abs."

Pulling back, unbuttoning his shirt, he chuckled. "You won't let me live that down, will you?"

"No plans to," she breathed in a husky admission as he finished with the last button. Impatient, she pushed the material back, off his shoulders and down his arms, letting her fingers trace over the bulging muscles in his arms.

She'd touched him before, his shoulders, his arms, but always with his clothes on. Seeing him shirtless, touching his bare skin, burned her alive.

"Are you real?" she asked, her voice catching. "You can't be."

"Real enough that I'm going to carry you to your bedroom and kiss you all over."

"Okay," she agreed, shivers covering her body at his words. "Hurry."

He laughed and scooped her up.

"Oh!" she squealed. "You didn't really have to carry me."

"Afraid I'll throw my back out and not be able to make good on my promise?"

"If you throw your back out then you just have to lie there. I'll do the work and you can just... lie there."

He groaned. A deep growl that came from low in his chest. "Sarah."

"Jude," she countered, wanting to say his name, to hear it on her lips. Jude. Her Jude. Hers.

Although Jude had never been inside her bedroom, he carried her straight there, laid her gently on her bed.

Staring up at him, Sarah waited on his next move.

"This is what you want? Once we do this, there's no going back," he reminded her yet again.

Was he kidding?

"I don't want to go back. I want you." To prove her point she reached for the shirt she wore and lifted the hem upward, glad when Jude helped pull the material free from her body, exposing the underwear her new BFF at the mall, Cher, had suggested.

She didn't boast any phenomenal curves, but beneath Jude's hot gaze Sarah felt sexy, beautiful, feminine.

"I'm almost afraid to touch you."

"We're going to have a major problem if you don't get over that," she warned, her eyes feasting on him.

"Noted." He undid her pants, slid the material over her hips, down her thighs. He sucked in a breath when he took in the barely there black lace that didn't begin to cover her bottom.

"Sarah," he groaned, tossing the material onto her bedroom floor. "No granny panties for you."

Heat rushed into her cheeks. Yep, she'd be sending Cher tickets to that concert she'd mentioned wanting to attend for having insisted Sarah buy underwear to go with her rapidly expanding new wardrobe.

"I feel as if I've waited for this forever."

"You have." Or maybe it was her who'd been waiting for this forever.

When he undid his pants, pulled them off and, rather than crawl into the bed beside her, instead tugged her around to where her bottom was at the edge of the bed, he lowered to kiss her throat, her chest, her belly, lower, yeah, Sarah was feeling forever.

Forever and ever and ever.

Oh, my.

CHAPTER TWELVE

JUDE WASN'T SURE how sexually inexperienced Sarah was, but she'd told him she'd never been kissed the way he'd kissed her that first time. So at best she'd had a less than pleasurable sexual encounter, but he suspected she'd not even done that.

Which was why he paced himself.

Because what he really wanted was to be inside her.

Deep inside her. Surrounded by her. Lost in her. Sarah.

Her whimpers of pleasure, her arches into his touch, her fingers curling into the quilt below her. Never had he experienced such pleasure at watching a woman, at giving pleasure.

He wanted to give Sarah everything. Every nuance of physical delight, emotional delight, everything.

When she looked back, thought of this night, he wanted only memories of perfection. He hadn't wanted her questioning anything, not him, not other women, nothing.

He wanted to be the entire focus of her world.

He was. He felt it in her touch, her kiss, the way she looked at him.

"Sarah?"

Her eyes opened. "Please."

Please. Such a hot word.

He trembled.

Not content to wait on him, Sarah reached for his waist, tugged on his boxers. "Now."

"Now?" Had that hoarse crackling sound been his voice?

She nodded.

Jude shucked his boxer briefs, covered Sarah while supporting his weight so he didn't squash her. He stared down into her lovely eyes and thought he was the luckiest man alive. Had to be. Because the way Sarah was looking at him made him so.

"Don't forget you're a safety guy," she reminded him.

A condom had been the last thing on Jude's mind.

How could he have forgotten something so

crucial, something meant to protect himself and Sarah? Because she made him feel safe in ways that had nothing to do with her lack of sexual experience?

No matter the reason, he shouldn't have forgotten. It was his job to protect her.

Always.

Even from him. Shifting his weight to one side, he reached with the other to find his pants, to maneuver the condom out of his pocket, to tear it open while praying that when he looked back into Sarah's eyes reality hadn't set in, that she hadn't changed her mind about them. About him.

Because he was one hundred percent positive he didn't deserve to be with her.

That he didn't deserve the gift she was about to give him. Maybe that's why he'd had to wait so long, so he could give something to her even if that something was simply the new confidence she exuded in herself, in her femininity.

When he met her gaze, relief filled him.

Her desire hadn't waned. She. Wanted. Him.

"This is your first time, isn't it, Sarah?"

A brief moment of hesitation flickered on her face, then she nodded.

His heart slammed against his ribcage. "I don't want to hurt you."

Trust shining in her eyes, she smiled. "You won't."

"I will," he acknowledged, wishing there was a way he could take her pain instead. "But I'll make it up to you. I promise."

Still smiling, she touched his face in what he could only call a caress.

"I know, Jude. That's why you're here."

Making sure she was really as ready as he believed she was, he groaned at the wet heat his fingers encountered. "Sarah."

She strained upward, cradled his face, and kissed him, deep, intense, fully. He kissed her back, catching her cry when he pushed inside with more restraint than he'd have believed he had, almost bursting from the intensity of what was happening between the two of them.

Sex had never been like this.

This giving, this taking, this explosion from the inside out. Physical explosion. Mental explosion. Emotional explosion.

Afterward, as he cradled her in his arms, he was

pretty sure there was nothing he wouldn't do for this woman, nothing he wouldn't give her.

She raised a sleepy head to smile. "That was worth waiting for."

Loving how she was looking at him with such happiness, he kissed her forehead. "Agreed. Get some rest because if you're able, I'm going to want you again. Soon."

Her eyes widened. "Really?"

"Is that your new favorite word?"

"Sex is my new favorite word," she corrected, then shook her head. "No, not sex. Orgasm. Orgasms is my new favorite word. Orgasms because that's what you did."

Jude swallowed, thinking she'd better be quiet because he was starting to stir in places that should be content for some time after what they'd done not so long before.

Tilting her head, she gave him a saucy little grin. "Do you think you can do that every time or was it a one-time deal because it was my first time?"

"Only one way to know for sure."

"That's what I figured," she mused, running her fingertip down his chest and into the groove along the center of his abdominal muscles, his ab muscles that had tightened into hard knots. Every muscle in him was hard. He was hard.

"You shouldn't do that," he warned. "You can't."

Her eyes widened in alarm. "I can't?"

"Not this quick."

She frowned. "Why not?"

"You'll be sore tomorrow," he reminded her.

"Is that all?" She shrugged her slim shoulders. "Then I guess you better make it worth it tonight."

Jude did.

"Charles and Grace got engaged!" Sarah gushed out the moment she burst into Jude's kitchen, her hair still wet from the bath he'd insisted she take while he made them breakfast.

He winced. He should have known Sarah would hear the news about Charles proposing to Grace on a sleigh ride in Central Park. Clearly, avoiding conversations about his cousin was going to be difficult over the next few days.

"I heard."

"Isn't it wonderful?" Sarah rushed on, her smile bright. "He sounded so happy when he called a few minutes ago."

Charles had called to tell her?

"That's nice."

"They love each other very much. It's so obvious when you see the two of them together."

"If you say so." Distracted, he lifted the pan lid to check their breakfast. Trapped steam rose and burned his fingers. Jude swore. "Can we not talk about Charles?"

So excited about the news, Sarah was oblivious to his mood and kept on talking. "He invited me to an impromptu engagement party Vanessa is throwing for them tonight."

Apparently, they did have to talk about his cousin.

Not looking at Sarah, Jude let out a long sigh. "How about those Knicks?"

"You must be happy for Charles, surely?"

"We're really not that close but, sure, I'm happy for him." Was he? Jude wasn't so sure.

"You're going to the party, too?"

Vanessa had called him just moments before. The news that Charles had asked Grace to marry him had shocked Jude. Had thrown him for a loop.

"No, I'm not going." When she looked ready to argue, he added, "Let it go, Sarah."

Unfortunately, she wasn't ready to let the matter drop.

"Why does it matter to you that I'm not going, anyway?"

Her gaze narrowed. "Maybe you weren't paying attention, but I was invited. I'd like to have a date."

"So you want to use me?" He was trying to lighten the conversation, to ease the annoyance he'd never heard in her voice before. To just spend the day with her and not think about Charles and Grace…and Nina.

"Absolutely." Sarah didn't crack a smile. "You found me out. That's all last night was. I was using you so I wouldn't have to go to Charles's engagement party alone."

"You're a terrible liar, Sarah."

"So are you," she countered, lifting her chin a notch.

He took a deep breath.

"I'm going whether you do or not," Sarah informed him, her disappointment thick. "Because I care about Charles and I want him to know how happy I am for them. Since no one but Penny knows about us, at least I'll be spared having to make excuses about why you aren't with me."

Did she really think no one knew about them except Penny? His father had called to ask about the woman Penny had flown around. His father hadn't asked him about the opposite sex in years. Fussed about how many women came in and out of Jude's life, yes, but never asked for details. Until Sarah. Which made Jude wonder what Penny had said. No doubt she'd sensed Sarah was special, that Jude wanted to make her happy, that he didn't want to disappoint her.

As he was doing by refusing to go to his cousin's engagement party.

"Is that it? Do you not want to go to Charles and Grace's party because you don't want your family to know about us?"

Old insecurities had appeared in her eyes and gutted Jude.

"They know."

More uncertainty flitted across her face. "Does that bother you?"

"No, and no, that they know about us is not why I'm not going to Vanessa's party."

Taking a deep breath, Sarah took his hand into hers and squeezed it tight. "Please, go, Jude. I can't imagine being with your family if they know about us and you aren't with me."

He opened his mouth to say no again, but his gaze met hers, saw the vulnerability in the depths, and when his mouth opened, the wrong words came out.

"I'll go."

"Really?" She practically leaped into his arms.

Jude wanted to take back those wrong words, but couldn't.

Not with how happy his mistake had made Sarah, but hell if he relished the prospect of seeing his cousin after all this time.

"You look absolutely stunning."

Sarah smiled at Jude's cousin Penny. "That's because you're comparing me to the pale, terrified woman who climbed into your helicopter."

Penny laughed. "You were stunning that night, too, but there's something different about you tonight."

Yeah, there was. Jude had introduced her to what all the fuss was about. The *ahhhh* of why people had sex, why sex sold things, why sex made the world go round and round and round.

He'd made her world go round and round.

She understood why Brandy had begged for more. Understood the constant flow of women in and out of Jude's apartment. When a man was that superb at giving pleasure, who cared if he was just using you?

Only not once had Jude made her feel that way.

Was she delusional?

Could a man like Jude fall for a woman like her?

He hadn't said he loved her, but when he looked at her…

Good grief, she was delusional.

Or something far worse. In love.

She lifted her gaze to Penny's and, unable to hide her surprise, her thoughts, Penny's eyes widened with realization, then a big grin cut across her beautiful face.

"Maybe we'll be celebrating another engagement soon."

Embarrassed that she'd revealed so much to Jude's cousin, Sarah shook her head in quick denial. "Jude isn't a settling-down kind of man."

Penny studied her. "But you'd like him to be?"

Sarah took a deep breath. "My guess is that every woman who has experienced your cousin's attention wants him to be the settling-down kind. He's a great man."

Penny nodded. "Until I saw him with you, I didn't think he'd ever be the settling-down kind either. He's had this restlessness about him. When he called to ask about showing you the city, that restlessness wasn't there. Something else was."

Don't let this go to your head, Sarah. Don't read too much into what Penny is saying. Just don't.

"What?" she whispered, knowing her heart was on her sleeve.

"Excitement. Hope." Penny shrugged. "Anticipation? You tell me. Whatever it is, it looks good on him."

Sarah glanced at where Jude talked with his father, an older version of Jude. "I've yet to find anything that doesn't look good on him."

Penny laughed. "You have it bad."

Sarah didn't bother to deny it. Why bother? She did have it bad.

"Lucky for you that he's just as smitten. Congrats."

Sarah knew it was way too early in her and Jude's relationship for anyone to be issuing congrats, but Penny's words fueled hope. Whatever was between them, she was different from any other woman he'd been with.

He'd shown her she was and she believed him.

He glanced toward her, and she smiled, letting everything in her heart shine because there was no point in trying to hide how she felt.

She was crazy about Jude.

Unfortunately, he didn't smile back. Or respond in any way other than to turn back to his father.

Okay, not what she was expecting, but maybe they were having an unpleasant conversation.

Only when she joined him a few minutes later, after he'd finished talking to his father and was finally alone, he was still scowling.

And abrupt in his responses.

Almost angry.

When another family member came over to talk to him, he dismissed them just as abruptly. Good grief, what was wrong with him?

Taking her arm, he gently guided her away from the crowd to where they stood off by themselves.

"Finally, I can breathe," he practically growled.

He hadn't had any problems with crowds on their other public outings, quite the opposite, so Sarah just stared, not sure what to say or do. She wanted to comfort him, but he didn't look welcoming of anything she might say or do.

"Remind me how you convinced me to come to this damn party again?"

Ouch.

Annoyed at his growl, hurt at his accusatory question, confused at his attitude, she lifted her chin and fake smiled. "How could you forget? I held a gun to your head this morning until you finally gave in and said you'd go for fear of your life."

His eyes flashed quicksilver. "Not funny."

"Yeah, well, neither is your attitude tonight."

"There is nothing wrong with my attitude. I told you from the beginning, I don't want to be here."

"So you're determined to make everyone have a bad time?"

"Are you having a bad time?" he snarled. "You seem to be buzzing from one person to the next and are all smiles."

Who was this stranger who'd taken hold of the sweet man she'd awakened next to that morning?

"Did I miss something?" she asked, totally confused. "You don't want me to smile or have a good time?"

He closed his eyes, raked his fingers through his hair, then took a deep breath. "I want you to have a good time." His tone wasn't thrilled, but at least he hadn't growled. "I was just ready to leave before we got here."

"I'd never have guessed."

"Normally, I appreciate that sharp wit of yours, but at the moment you'll have to excuse me." He glanced around the room, almost desperately. "I'm going to go find something to drink. You want something?"

Yeah, she wanted the man she'd made love to back and this belligerent stranger gone.

Not that he waited for her to answer.

She watched him walk away, watched as people came over to talk to him. He shifted his weight, didn't make eye contact, and just looked awkward.

What was wrong with him?

CHAPTER THIRTEEN

COMING HERE HAD been a mistake.

Jude had thought going to Charles and Grace's engagement party would be okay, that he could deal with seeing his cousin.

He'd been wrong.

He'd rather be in the middle of a burning building than in the same room as Charles.

Time hadn't changed that.

Jude supposed it never would.

He finished talking to family member after family member who cornered him on his way to get his drink, and finally made it back to where Sarah patiently waited. He'd felt her watching him, and he'd bristled, not wanting her to see beneath the surface. Not that the surface was shiny and attractive.

Far from it. But what was beneath was bitter and hurt and didn't want to be in this room full of partygoers.

"Are you embarrassed to be here with me?"

He cut his gaze to her. Why had he said he'd come? He should have let her come and been sitting in his apartment, watching the sunset over the city. That would have been relaxing, enjoyable, pleasant, not this.

"You know that's not the case," he finally said, wishing she'd say she wanted to go home.

"Then why are you acting so weird?"

Because seeing Charles laughing, touching another woman—her hand, her back, her face—and looking at another woman with love felt all kinds of wrong. Felt like a betrayal to Nina.

How could he? Nina had loved Charles. Had died giving birth to his twins.

Had broken Jude's heart.

Charles had moved on, was in love with Grace, was going to raise Nina's children with Grace, was happy.

His cousin had found genuine joy in life again.

Joy in love again.

Which made Jude itch to escape because he knew how quickly that joy could be ripped away.

Being here felt wrong, felt like a betrayal to Nina's memory, like a betrayal to himself.

Maybe last night with Sarah had initiated that sense of betrayal, of guilt.

He'd been with other women, but they'd meant nothing.

Sarah meant something.

A whole lot of something.

That scared the hell out of him.

He wanted away from this party.

Everyone was celebrating love and happiness. Had Charles forgotten how quickly that could change?

How quickly how all hope could disappear?

Not that Nina had loved Jude. Not as more than a friend.

Neither did he fool himself that Sarah loved him.

She cared for him. He saw it in her eyes, but this was all new to her, and she was enamored with the sexual bliss they gave each other.

"Don't say you aren't acting weird, because you have no clue what I just asked you," she interrupted his thoughts.

"You asked why I was acting weird," he countered, feeling a little off kilter inside.

"Yeah, three questions ago." She gave a little shake of her head. "This is your family, Jude. Your amazing, wonderful family who are glad you are here, who want to talk to you and spend time with you. Smile."

"If you like them so much, you can have them."

"I wish." Realizing what she'd said, Sarah turned a bright shade of red. "That could be taken in all kinds of wrong ways, so let me clarify that I just meant I wish I had a big loving family like yours. Not that I was implying I specifically wanted your family to be mine."

Well, as long as they were straight on that.

"They're not all they're cracked up to be," he assured her, taking a long drink from his glass.

"At least they're family and they love you."

Not wanting to talk about his family anymore and knowing he was digging a hole he didn't want to be in, Jude changed the direction of their conversation. "Do you not have family, Sarah? Is that what this is about?"

Her face a little pale, she shrugged. "My mother lives in Queens."

She'd mentioned her mother a few times, briefly, but no one else.

"What about the rest of your family?"

"There is no rest of my family," she told him,

toying with the diamond earrings he'd given her on the night he'd taken her to the Broadway show. Why had he done that? He'd not bought jewelry for a woman ever.

"My mother ran off with her boyfriend when she was sixteen and lost all contact with her parents. If they are still alive, I've no clue. Apparently, she contacted them a few times early on, but they'd written her off as dead and refused to let her back into their lives. When she told them she had a baby, they wanted nothing to do with me, telling her she'd made her bed and to lie in it. Over the years, she worked about every kind of job there is, usually waitressing. Until she got involved with some loser again, that is, and then we'd end up in a homeless shelter or at one of her coworkers' homes until she could save up enough to get us back off the streets again."

He'd gotten the impression she'd come from humble beginnings, but he hadn't realized the scope of Sarah's childhood, of what she'd had to overcome to achieve those academic scholarships she'd mentioned.

"She lives in a group home for abused women. I used to offer to let her live with me, but she never would. She leaves the home from time to time, but always goes back. This last time, she took a job at the shelter. It suits her. She feels safe there with other women who hate men."

A bit stunned she'd revealed so much in the midst of a party, Jude stared. Yet again, this woman amazed him. He wanted to take her into his arms, protect her from the world, and tell her how proud he was, but she was as bristly now as he'd been minutes before.

"So, yeah, your big, loud, but loving family looks pretty good to me because it's something I've never had and grew up dreaming of." Every word dripped disapproval of his behavior.

"I'm sorry," he said, and meant.

"Don't be. Just appreciate what you have, because I don't believe you do."

"I like my family."

She looked him straight in the eyes and asked a question that told him she saw further beneath the surface than any other person ever had. "Just not Charles?"

The question, the answer, gutted him.

"I don't want to talk about Charles."

Because seeing Charles reminded Jude of how

quickly everything could change, of how he had so much guilt over everything that had happened after he'd lost Nina to his cousin.

Sarah's lips pursed with disappointment. In him. He didn't like it.

"Like I've said before," she continued, not backing away from the subject despite his desire that she would, "Charles is an excellent man, an excellent boss and doctor. He's a fabulous father and just look at how he is with Grace." She cast a longing glance toward the couple. "I've met few better men in my life and none I admire more, especially at the moment."

Which was a direct dig at him. Jude bristled.

"With the way you talk about him," he barked, full of dislike at both her words and the way she was looking toward his cousin, "I'm surprised you didn't sleep with him instead of me."

It was a low blow. Jude knew it was a low blow. He'd like to retract the stupid words, but couldn't.

Staring at him in wide-eyed horror, Sarah's jaw dropped. "Did you really just say that?"

Yeah, he had. He shouldn't have. His words had been crass and hateful and stupid.

What was wrong with him?

He'd felt like the luckiest man on earth right up until Vanessa had called him. How could going to a party to celebrate Charles's engagement throw him so far off center?

Make his head cloudy and old hurt, old fears, abound?

Or was it how happy he'd been a few hours ago that was getting muddled up with the past that was messing with his head?

"While you think about what you just said, I'm going to give my congratulations to Charles and Grace." With that quiet scolding, Sarah gave him another disapproving look, then walked over to hug Grace and kiss Charles on the cheek.

Jealousy erupted within Jude the likes of which he'd never known. Irrational jealousy because he knew Sarah wasn't attracted to Charles.

He also knew that Charles was in love with Grace.

Yet jealousy blinded him.

Just as it had before he'd opened his mouth and spewed stupidity.

Blinded him.

To rational thought.

To reason.

To everything.

He found himself behaving with even more stupidity, because before he knew it he was at Sarah's side, wishing his cousin and Grace a mumbled congrats, then guiding Sarah away from the party.

"We're leaving."

She squared her shoulders and looked ready to insist on staying. She must have seen the finality in his demand because she narrowed her gaze and said, "Fine."

The taxi ride to their apartments was silent. Not a silence of gleeful anticipation as it had been the night before, but just stone-cold quiet that dug more and more distance between them.

Sarah was upset and well within her rights to be.

He was acting like a jerk, knew it, but couldn't seem to rein in whatever devil drove his lapse into insanity.

When they reached their apartment doors, she didn't look to him in question, just took out her key and let herself into her apartment. She didn't invite him in, but left the door wide open, so he followed.

She dropped her coat, bag, and scarf onto the sofa, then turned. "Okay, we're away from that 'damn party'. I think it's time you tell me what is going on between you and your cousin."

"What makes you think you have a right to demand anything of me?"

She flinched and Jude hated his words, hated that he'd hurt her. Again. Hated that he felt the way he did, that his insides were black.

Could betrayal and guilt eat away a man's reason?

"Fine. No arguments from me. I have no rights where you are concerned." She gestured to the door they'd just walked through. "Leave."

Pain ripped through him. He shut his eyes. "Don't."

"Don't? Are you kidding me? Don't?" She practically screamed. At least it felt that way. In reality, her voice wasn't much higher than normal. It was her tone, the hurt, the anger, the seething, the fear and uncertainty, the total disillusionment, all negatives that he'd caused.

Just as he had with Nina. The argument they'd had rushed through his mind. He'd been a jerk then, too, when Nina had tried to salvage their friendship.

He wasn't good at this relationship thing. Maybe that was why he did one-night stands.

No, he knew why he did one-night stands.

That had been abundantly clear when he'd seen Charles. He didn't want to get attached, to care again, ever.

Because he didn't want to get hurt, again.

He used Nina as a shield, a defense, a reminder to never let himself care.

He'd failed.

He cared about Sarah.

He didn't want an argument to be his last conversation with Sarah as it had been with Nina.

Which was why he was going to have to admit some things he'd never admitted to anyone, never said out loud.

"Don't make me go," he began. When she looked ready to toss him out anyway, he rushed on. "At least, not without letting me explain."

"You owe me no explanations," she bit out, her gaze shooting daggers. "We've already established that."

He'd done that, caused her anger, her lashing out, and he deserved her to toss him out rather than hear him.

"I shouldn't have said what I did, Sarah."

"Actually, you should have, because I'd gotten everything all tangled up in my head and thought you actually had feelings for me, that I was different from the female parade coming out of your bedroom. Ha," she scoffed, pacing across the room and shaking her head in dismay. "What a fool I was."

"You weren't a fool."

"I wasn't smart."

He took a deep breath and said what had to be said to break through her ire and disillusionment.

"I was in love with Charles's wife."

As he'd expected, Sarah's expression changed, went from hurt and angry to stunned.

"What?"

"I loved Nina." There. He'd said it. Admitted the truth out loud. For the first time ever.

To Sarah.

Probably not the best person to admit that particular truth to, but he'd never been tempted to tell anyone else. Besides, how else could he explain his unacceptable behavior at Charles and Grace's engagement party? To make Sarah understand the dark swirling emotions inside him?

She stared, wide-eyed and with a mixture of pity and abhorrence. "But that's…"

"I introduced Nina to Charles. I brought her to a party with me and was showing her off to my family, thinking our friendship was blossoming into something straight out of a fairy tale. Instead, I got to watch as I introduced my cousin, as she blushed, as she looked at him with an excitement in her eyes that had never shown there when she looked at me. I watched while the woman I was planning to spend the rest of my life with fell all over herself for my cousin, that 'most excellent man', as you call him."

Maybe he shouldn't have thrown Sarah's description of Charles at her, but the words spewed from his mouth.

"I got to watch while she married him, while they shared excitement over their announcement they were going to be parents. I got to grieve in silence when she died giving birth to his children and to fall apart later, in private, when I could let out the pain in my heart. So you'll understand that seeing my cousin fawn over another woman, betraying Nina's memory, then listening to you go on about him, well, tonight wasn't the best of nights."

"Why did you say you'd go?" Sarah whispered, dropping against the back of the sofa, as if her legs would no longer support her.

Good question. Why had he agreed to something so idiotic?

"Because you wanted me to," he said truthfully. Maybe he'd also wanted to see Charles and Grace with his own eyes, because he hadn't quite been able to believe Charles could love again after Nina. Jude's insides shook more than a little as he continued. "You gave me something precious and I wanted to give you something you wanted. Agreeing to go to that party was the only thing I knew that you wanted from me."

Jude had felt guilty that he'd taken Sarah's virginity, had felt obligated to give her something in return, had decided not to make her suffer through another party as the odd man, woman, out.

Great.

If Sarah had known how the night would unfold, she'd have begged him not to go.

Because now so much made sense.

Jude wasn't in love with her. She wasn't the one.

He was in love with a ghost.

Nina Davenport.

Sarah remembered the woman, had always understood why Charles had so completely loved her. She'd been beautiful, gracious, kind, intelligent, and had glowed with happiness. Sarah remembered how much joy Nina had shone with at her pregnancy, how she'd vocalized her happiness that she and Charles were going to be parents, how everyone at the hospital had mourned her unexpected death after the twins had been born. How Charles had grieved his loss.

Somewhere in the privacy of the playboy persona he exuded to the world, Jude had been grieving his loss, too.

Because he'd been in love with Nina.

Was still in love with her.

Sarah could hear it in his voice, in the pain that was still so very raw.

"I… I don't know what to say."

"I don't expect you to say anything." He raked his fingers through his hair, glancing around her living room without really looking. "I just felt you needed to know why tonight was the way it was." He closed his eyes. "Why I'm the way I am."

Her heart pounded in her chest at the gravity of their conversation, at all the implications of his admission, of all her silly hopes and dreams that had taken life over the past few days and how they'd come crashing back to cold, harsh reality. She'd known better. She had. Stupid, silly her. A lifetime of preaching from her mother and yet a few flirty words from a sexy neighbor and she'd gone all stupid. Had gone from being content with her successful career to thinking maybe she could have more.

She swallowed her wounded pride and shook her head. "You failed, then, because I don't understand your behavior any more now than I did then. Nina is gone. Charles has every right to love again. It's what she would have wanted him to do."

"I know that."

"But you blame him that he has?"

He hesitated just long enough that, no matter what words came out, Sarah knew the real answer.

"It's obvious you do. Because you can't move on, you condemn Charles because he has." She didn't need a degree to know that she'd hit the nail on the head. Jude was still in love with Nina and seeing Charles happy had undone him. "Maybe you need counseling."

"I don't need counseling."

"Having sex with half the females in Manhattan hasn't cured you."

His gaze narrowed. "I don't need counseling."

"You're grieving another man's wife. You need something."

"She wasn't his wife when I fell in love with her," he reminded her, sounding defensive. "She didn't even know him."

"She chose him."

"You say that as if you think I don't know that." Anger laced his words. "You think I don't? I lived it every single day. It doesn't matter now."

"Sure it does. You're still living it." She said the words softly, but they echoed around the room as if she'd screamed them from a speaker phone.

Jude opened his mouth to say more, but his cell-phone rang.

It wasn't a normal ring but the specially programmed one that she'd never heard but which he'd warned her about. It meant there was an emergency that required him to get to the fire hall as soon as possible.

He pulled his phone out, glanced at it as if he considered ignoring the call, which surprised her, but then let out a resigned sigh as he touched the screen to answer.

Which was just as well.

There was no reason for him to ignore the call. He was in love with a ghost and Sarah couldn't compete with a dead woman. Competing with the beauty queens he usually dated had been intimidating enough. Competing with the memory of lovely Nina Davenport, well, that didn't even tempt.

Jude loved Nina.

Those three little words summarized everything. There was nothing else that needed to be said. Or done.

He hung up his phone. "I've got to go, but this conversation isn't over."

He was wrong. It was over.

They were over.

He was in love with another woman.

Maybe that wouldn't matter to some women, but it mattered to Sarah. She wasn't going to have sex with a man, have a relationship of any kind with a man, knowing that he loved another woman, that he'd given his heart to a woman who hadn't even wanted it, and that Sarah would always be second best, if she was even that.

Maybe when she'd started this she'd had no real expectations from him, but over the past few weeks, expectations had sprouted roots and blossomed. Expectations that, no matter how much she hoped and prayed, could never be met because the man she'd fallen for loved a woman who would never grow old, would never falter or mess up, because she was eternalized in his mind as the perfect woman. Even in real life, Nina had been as close to that as a living breathing woman came.

Sarah couldn't compete with that. She wouldn't.

Better to cut her losses now and move on before she became so entangled with Jude that she couldn't function without him, before every warning her mother had ever preached came to be.

He must have seen that truth in her eyes, because rather than leave he hesitated. "Sarah, I—"

"Please, don't." She stopped him. "There's no need. We both got what we wanted and there's nothing more that needs to be said. Not from you and not from me."

"I disagree. I—"

"You need to go," she reminded him. "Goodbye."

They both knew she meant for more than just the moment.

Still, he hesitated, then seemed to accept the reality of whether it was now or Christmas, as he'd previously suggested, they would be saying goodbye. Apparently he agreed now was as good a time as any, because he nodded.

"If that's how you feel. Bye, Sarah."

With that, he left. No goodbye kiss, no hug, no "It's been fun", nothing. Just bye.

Sarah stared at the door, waiting for the tears, waiting for the misery to rip at her chest and tear her to bits. It was coming. She could feel it.

Oh, she'd survive. She'd move on. She'd go back to her rather mundane existence, but on the inside she'd never be quite the same.

Thinking Manhattan would forever be changed as well, she walked over to her floor-to-ceiling view of the city, meaning to stare out, to draw comfort from what usually filled her with inner peace, but instead her reflection in the glass caught her eye.

The reflection that was very different from that of the drab woman who'd done her best to blend into the background a mere three weeks ago.

No, she would not go back to her mundane existence.

She would live, would embrace life, would embrace the city she loved, and maybe if she got lucky, someday she would find someone who could love her the way Jude loved a woman who'd died years ago.

If not, she would still embrace the woman reflected back at her. She wouldn't hide herself away.

Not because of her mother's warnings, not because of bad dating experiences, not ever again.

She couldn't imagine ever wanting anyone the way she wanted Jude, but they said time healed all wounds. It looked as if she would be testing that theory.

The first tear rolled down her cheek. She didn't fight it, knew more were to follow, and they would have, except her phone buzzed.

Was it…? No, it couldn't be. Neither did she really want it to be. Even if he wanted to continue their affair, she couldn't. The longer she let this go on, the more difficult recovering would be. She'd done the right thing.

She walked to her purse, pulled out her phone. The hospital. That only meant one thing.

With Charles and Grace's engagement party, a lot of the ER staff were at the party so staffing was tight. Her phone wouldn't be ringing unless she was needed.

Just as well, a busy night in the emergency room would keep her distracted from her broken heart.

CHAPTER FOURTEEN

JUDE AND ROGER made their way up a stairwell, one of the few still accessible in the burning apartment complex.

It wasn't known yet what had started the fire in the older high-rise, but the fire had quickly escalated and now encompassed several floors.

More than a hundred people had been evacuated, but there were many more still missing. How many wasn't even known at this point. Several had called in to 911 and were trapped on a particular level where part of the floor above had caved in.

A communication center worker had been on the phone with an elderly lady in one of the apartments for about ten minutes prior to losing the connection.

They'd cleared out known victims on lower floors, getting them to the stairwell, then had been informed of the elderly couple and at least one other who were trapped a few floors above them.

Command hadn't ordered them out yet. "Yet" being the key word because it was coming. Roger and Jude had taken off up the stairwell that so far was still passable. Jude prayed it stayed that way, that they could use it to get the rest of the tenants out.

At least two had died in the fire already. Jude didn't want there to be a third added to that number and Lord forbid more than that.

But this building had him on high alert. Not that he wasn't with every fire, but tonight every instinct told him he shouldn't be there.

Probably his stupid heart whining that he'd walked away from Sarah.

That he'd left with Sarah thinking that he was still in love with Nina.

He wasn't.

He wasn't in love with Nina.

How freeing it was to think that. To know that.

He was no longer in love with a woman he could never have.

At least, he hoped he wasn't.

Because the walls Sarah had been throwing between them tonight sure weren't reassuring. Far, far from it.

How quickly she'd thrown their relationship away.

That bothered him.

But it was his own fault.

She believed he was in love with another woman. A woman she couldn't fight against or even think ill of.

But she believed wrong.

He had loved Nina. In some ways, he still loved her and always would. But he wasn't in love with her. When he'd stopped and the guilt over their argument, over the strain on his relationship with Charles, had taken over, he wasn't sure. Years ago. Perhaps even before she'd died, although he'd not realized it at the time because he'd been so hurt, so caught up in the idea of being in love with Nina that he'd not let himself see the truth.

Until Sarah had forced him to see the truth.

In such a short time she'd come into his life and turned his whole world upside down.

Made everything brighter, clearer, better.

"Man, watch what you are doing," Roger warned, when Jude reached for a doorway without checking it first with the thermal imaging camera. "Don't open that until we know what's behind it."

Yeah, he knew that.

He also knew he needed to get his brain in gear until they got out of this death trap. Being distracted wasn't doing Roger or him any favors.

He checked the door for heat, determined that the hallway was passable so they could get to the known trapped elderly couple and check for any additional trapped victims. Getting low, he opened the door and they made their way into the smoke-filled hallway.

Knowing which apartment the elderly couple had called in to the emergency communication center from, Jude and Roger made their way there as quickly as possible. Their door was unlocked, but the woman had wisely stuffed towels around the floor, which helped keep the smoke out of their apartment, but made opening the door more difficult.

Time was of the essence.

Jude used his shoulder, and shoved hard against the door. It gave and he went flying into the room. Quickly, they located the elderly couple hunched in a bathtub and cleared a path to them.

The man had fallen and injured his leg while trying to get them out. Unwilling to leave him, his wife had managed to drag him back into the apartment on a sheet, pulled him into the bathroom, and somehow gotten him into the tub. She'd pushed towels up around the doorway, trying to keep the smoke out, and they'd huddled together, thinking they were probably going to burn alive.

A hellish feeling for sure.

Thank God, they'd found them.

Roger called for back-up and to check the accessibility of the stairwell they'd come up. It was still open and help to get the Johnsons out of the building was on its way.

Unfortunately, Clara Johnson said there were more people trapped on their floor.

"Betty Kingston lives two doors down. I called her earlier, when I got Ed back to the bathroom," the woman fretted, looking as if she might drop from stress and exhaustion any moment. "She said part of her ceiling had collapsed in front of her door. I told her we were in the tub and that's where she was going, too. To her tub."

Two doors down.

"There's another couple who live in the corner

apartment. Stanley and Estelle Miller," Mrs. Johnson continued. "Betty said they have to be trapped, too, because the part of her ceiling that caved in knocked part of the wall down with it and would have blocked them in, too, if they weren't already out." The woman gave Jude a horrified look. "What if they aren't out?"

Jude glanced at Roger.

"On it," his best friend said, calling down to Command to see if a Betty Kingston or the Miller couple had been located.

As they'd feared, neither had.

Jude grabbed Mr. Johnson, having the man hold on around his neck. Roger took hold of Mrs. Johnson.

"This is quite embarrassing, you know," Mr. Johnson mumbled.

"I bet you've experienced worse." Despite the severity of the situation, Jude grinned as they made their way back into the hallway. Smoke billowed thickly, so he got low, having Mr. Johnson hold onto his back as he hunkered down and moved them as quickly as possibly down the hallway and toward the emergency stairwell.

"Yeah, when that blasted woman of mine dragged

me into the bathroom and refused to leave me, despite me begging her to go save herself."

"Helluva woman you got there."

"Don't think I don't know it."

The man coughed so fiercely Jude feared he was going to have to stop moving and beat on the man's back.

"Sixty-one years and I'm grateful for every day of her stubbornness driving me crazy."

"I understand."

"You got a stubborn woman, too?"

"Oh, yeah. Stubborn and smart. Sarah's a doctor. Works in the emergency room at Manhattan Mercy so you may meet her to get that leg checked before the night is up."

Before they got out of the hallway, the heat had intensified, as had the smoke.

Finally, they made their way to the stairwell and carried the couple down the flights until they met up with other crew.

Other crew who wanted to go the rest of the way up and get out the other missing people.

"We already know the layout of the apartments and where the one woman is hiding. Take the Johnsons down, get them to safety. We'll get the others."

At least the ones on that floor. Others from their crew and from several stations around that section of Manhattan were working other floors in the building, fighting the fire, trying to keep it contained and from spreading to the cracker box apartment buildings that were all around. This fire could easily get out of control and take out the entire block. Or worse.

"Thank you," Mr. Johnson said as he transferred to the other firefighter. "You want me to put in a good word for you if I run across your Sarah?"

"Yeah, if you run across Dr. Sarah Grayson, you do that. Tell her I'm sorry and that I'm crazy about her, while you're at it," Jude called, as he took back off up the stairwell, Roger close on his heels.

Jude and Roger made their way back to the floor, back down the smoke-filled hallway, and had to bust into Betty Kingston's apartment using their axes.

Fortunately, they rescued the terrified frail little woman from right where Clara Johnson had said they'd find her. Her tub. She'd inhaled a lot of smoke and was slightly asphyxiated, but otherwise appeared okay.

Except that she was too weak to make her way

out of the apartment. Which wouldn't be a problem, except Ms. Kingston wasn't the only victim still on the floor.

"The Millers," the woman said, amidst a hacking coughing spell.

They needed to get her out, but get to the other couple, too. The other couple they weren't even for sure were there, but who might be trapped in the apartment next to Ms. Kingston's. The woman certainly was convinced they were in the apartment.

"Let's get her to the stairwell," Roger said. "We'll hand her over to back-up, then go back for the Millers."

As they made their way out into the floor hallway, they heard a crash from one of the apartments a few doors down from where they were. Not the apartment where the couple might be but close.

Just then the fire truck's horn blare could be heard above the fire. Once. Twice. Again.

Roger turned back, his gaze meeting Jude's. "Not this time, man. We've got to get out of here, and you know it. I've a bad feeling. This building is about to go."

Jude cursed.

"You're right," he said, knowing there was no time to waste. "Let's get out of here."

Roger's look of relief that Jude wasn't insisting they clear the other apartment was almost palpable.

Roger loaded up the woman and they made their way to the stairwell.

They were leaving a couple to die. A couple they were in fairly close proximity to.

Someone's family.

Someone's father, mother, sister, brother, cousin.

Cousin. Jude needed to apologize to his cousin.

To tell Charles he was sorry he'd shut him out of his life despite multiple efforts on Charles's part to heal whatever rift that had come between them.

Despite Nina's efforts to heal the rift.

Of course, Charles had never understood Jude's distancing himself. How could he have when he'd never known how Jude had felt about Nina?

Yeah, he needed to apologize to his cousin.

And to Sarah.

He needed to tell Sarah how he felt about her.

Sarah. Beautiful, sweet Sarah.

She might think their conversation was over, but he knew better, had known better when he'd left her apartment. If it took him the rest of his life, he'd make tonight up to her, would prove to her that he was a better man than the one he'd shown her at Charles and Grace's party.

He was a better man.

He was a man who did the right thing.

The right thing wasn't leaving a trapped elderly couple to burn alive.

Jude stopped, waited to make sure his partner made it to the stairwell, then saluted his friend, who had realized Jude wasn't immediately behind him and was shaking his head and mouthing all kinds of foul words.

Jude turned back to get the Millers.

A risky, foolish move. You didn't go off on your own in a burning building. You stayed with your partner for the safety of both of you.

His partner would do the right thing, too, would get Betty Kingston down those stairs and to safety. Roger would be all right. If all went as planned, Jude would have the Millers busted free and would be down those stairs with them before Roger had time to attempt coming back for him.

If Jude died in the process of making an exit for the Millers, then so be it.

There were worse things than laying your life down for others.

CHAPTER FIFTEEN

"EARLIER I MEANT to tell you how fabulous you looked, but now you look as tired as I feel after being here all day. You okay?"

Sarah glanced at Shelley. Fabulous wasn't how she'd have described herself at any point that evening. Well, prior to Jude and her arriving at the engagement party Sarah had felt a bit like a belle on her way to a ball. As if she'd been the star of the evening, shining for Jude.

Ha. If so, that star had burned out and now there was a painful gaping black hole where hope had once shone.

"Even before I got here, it had been a long night," she admitted, squirting hand sanitizer on her hands and rubbing them together as she readied to go to the next patient. "But I'm fine."

"It's just getting started. Sorry you got called away from Charles and Grace's party. Especially with as glam as you looked when you got here."

"I was in scrubs when I got here," she reminded her.

"Yeah, scrubs and make-up and a fancy hairdo. You looked like a movie star doctor."

"That's funny." But neither Sarah nor Shelley were laughing. Or dallying to talk as they quickly moved from one patient to the next.

"Hot date?"

Her date had been hot. He'd also been a jerk. And admitted he was in love with another woman. No biggie.

"I went out with my neighbor, but it wasn't a big deal. We're not dating."

Not anymore.

But for the past few weeks she'd felt...alive. Wonderfully, femininely alive.

The night before she'd felt amazingly alive in Jude's arms. Then, poof, he'd transformed into someone totally inconsistent with who she'd believed him to be.

Because he'd gotten what he'd wanted and was ready to move on?

He was usually a one-night-stand man, but maybe he'd given her a few weeks because she'd been a virgin?

He probably had treated her more delicately because of her inexperience, but she believed his reasons for his bad behavior. He'd been in love with Nina and had shut off a part of himself when she'd died, had shut himself off from his family.

On autopilot, Sarah treated another patient, deeming the young man's severe abdominal pain to be a renal stone.

Sending over a prescription to manage his pain until he could be seen by Nephrology in clinic, Sarah typed in discharge orders and stepped out of the bay.

The emergency department was crazily busy. People, both patients and hospital personnel, were everywhere. In addition to the usual influx of patients, an apartment building filled mainly with low-income elderly had caught fire. Two people were confirmed dead. Dozens more had been rescued and brought in for smoke inhalation and minor burns. The hospital was still on standby as more were trapped inside the building.

Last she'd heard the fire was running rampant and out of control.

Was Jude there?

Of course he was.

That had to be the emergency call he'd gotten right before he'd left her apartment.

He was there. Probably inside that burning building, risking everything for strangers.

Because that's what he did.

Risked everything for strangers.

That's why he had the steady flow of different women.

Because he wouldn't let anyone get close.

Why he had invested more time with her than he generally gave, she wasn't sure. No doubt he regretted having done so, regretted having admitted the truth.

Not that he had to worry that she'd tell Charles. Jude's secret was safe with her. It wasn't her place to try to heal the rift between the two cousins, or to try to get Jude the counseling he so obviously needed that he couldn't let go of a dead woman's memory.

He'd put Sarah in her place tonight.

Her place wasn't to interfere in his life in any shape, form, or fashion.

He didn't let anyone interfere in his life, not friends or family or women. He kept them all at a distance and preferred it that way.

"You okay?"

Sarah blinked at her nurse. "Fine."

"You zoned out on me for a few seconds. You've been running since you got here. You need a short break or a drink or something?"

Sarah shook her head. "Sorry. Got lost in my thoughts, but I'm fine. Who's next?"

Every bay was full of smoke inhalation victims. Some with burns, some not. Every respiratory therapist in the hospital was administering oxygen and nebulizer treatments and whatever else was needed to keep airways open. Fortunately, so far only a few had had to be intubated, but from the calls they were getting from EMS, more victims were on their way.

Other hospital personnel were talking to family members and less critical patients who they'd stuck in the waiting area, offering drinks, blankets, and just a comforting pat on the hand in some cases.

All the acutely critical had been seen to and were being appropriately cared for. Now Sarah and the other providers would start chipping away at the overflow of minor injuries and other anomalies that had sent folks into the emergency room on a Saturday night.

Or so she'd thought.

At that moment, a gurney came rushing in, with another close on its heels. An elderly man and an elderly woman.

Paul was the paramedic with the elderly man who appeared to be in worse shape than the woman on the second gurney. Both wore oxygen masks, but the woman kept taking hers off to talk to the paramedic pushing her.

They had no empty bay to put either of the new patients, but hopefully the kidney stone patient would be out of his room soon. Plus, the transport crew was on their way to admit another patient up to the medical floor. Goodness knew the emergency room was giving them a workout with so many more than normal admissions thanks to the smoke inhalation victims needing respiratory observation at least overnight.

Sarah rushed over to meet Paul since the elderly man appeared to be more critically injured. "There's not an empty bay. Let's pull him over this way so he's not in the direct line of traffic and you can give me report while I do my assessment."

"Ed Johnson and his wife, Clara…" Paul gestured over to the other gurney "…were trapped in their apartment bathroom. Like almost everyone brought in tonight, Ed is suffering from smoke inhalation, but his main injury is from a fall that occurred when he and his wife were trying to get out of the building."

"Tripped over my own two feet," the man said between coughs, his words muffled by his oxygen mask.

"His wife is a retired nurse and took a rolled-up bed sheet, put it under his arms, and dragged him back into their apartment. She blocked their doors with wet towels, and barricaded them in their bathroom where she called 911 and begged for help."

For a brief moment Sarah tried to imagine the pure terror the couple had to have felt. She shuddered.

"Thank God someone got to them."

Paul nodded, then a light dawned on his face. "Actually, it was my buddy, the one you met with the little girl a couple of weeks ago, who pulled them out."

"Jude?"

"That's him." Paul grinned. "Figured you'd remember him. He's that kind of guy."

Jude had rescued the couple, had saved their lives.

"Were they the last of the victims?" she asked, hopeful.

Paul's smile faded and he shook his head. "There were still others trapped. They'd called for everyone to evacuate the building as we loaded the ambulance with the Johnsons."

"Jude was out then?" she asked, praying that he'd heeded the warning.

Paul shook his head. "I don't think so. Like I told you before, that man is first one in and last one out." Paul finished giving report, then took off to get back to the fire scene, ready for the next load.

"Good man," her patient said through his oxygen mask after Paul had left.

"Paul? I only know him from coming into contact with him here, but, yes, he seems to be."

Mr. Johnson shook his head. "Didn't mean him."

It took Sarah a few seconds to realize Mr. Johnson meant Jude.

"I'm glad he got you out."

Mr. Johnson coughed so hard his oxygen sats dropped several points and Sarah began to wonder if she was going to have to suction, then intubate him.

When he finally cleared his throat, he grabbed Sarah's hand. "You're Dr. Sarah Grayson?"

She blinked in surprise. "I am."

"Said he was sorry."

"You must be…" She started to say "confused", but why else would Mr. Johnson say something of the sort unless Jude had indeed talked about her?

The question was why? Why would he say anything about her at all? Much less tell a virtual stranger that he was sorry?

"He said I might see you here." Mr. Johnson paused to cough and this time Sarah did suction him to clear the mucus from his throat.

When the man had caught his breath, he continued as if nothing had happened. "He told me if I saw you here to put in a good word and tell you he was sorry and that he was crazy about you."

Sarah's head spun. Jude had sent word to her? Why?

"He was going back for Betty Kingston. She was in her bathroom, too. Whole place was up in flames." The old man coughed again. "I hope he found Betty. And the Millers. And got out of that inferno."

Sarah's heart pounded. Jude was inside a burning building. He was in danger.

The thought gutted her. Made her want to call him and beg him to get out of the building if he wasn't already.

She closed her eyes, took a deep breath.

Examining Mr. Johnson, Sarah ended up admitting him to the medical floor and consulted orthopedic surgery. Bedside X-ray had shown he'd fractured his right hip when he'd fallen. Mrs. Johnson had suffered mild smoke inhalation and had been discharged. As Sarah expected, the woman stayed with her husband rather than leave.

Then again, her home had burned. She might not have anywhere else to go. Not that Sarah thought she'd leave even if she did.

Ambulances dropped off victims from a motor vehicle crash. Pedestrians came in with abdominal and chest pain. The ER stayed crazy. Sarah was swamped. But her heart wasn't fully on what she was doing.

Because no Betty Kingston or Millers had come into the emergency department and if they were who Jude had gone back for, surely they should be out by now? Should be in the emergency department, being given a good once-over even under the best of circumstances of being trapped inside a burning building.

Had Jude gotten them out?

Had Jude gotten out?

"Oh, God!" Shelley breathed, catching Sarah's attention. Her friend had just been at the unit desk and her face was pale. "That building that was on fire collapsed."

Collapsed.

Jude!

"Was everyone out?" she managed to squeak from her tight throat.

Shelley shook her head. "Per the call that just came in there were people still inside. Firefighters, too."

The room spun around, making Sarah think she might fall to her knees.

First one in. Last one out.

Wasn't that what Paul had said? Please, no.

Please, just, no.

"Sarah?"

Insides shaking, she stared at Shelley. "My neighbor works for the fire department."

"Your neighbor?"

Jude was so much more than her neighbor. He was...her heart.

Sarah's personal life never interfered with her work.

Never.

But for the life of her she couldn't focus.

Couldn't think.

Could only feel.

Jude.

"Sarah?"

"I...um...sorry. I'm feeling a little light-headed. I'm going to grab that drink, Shelley. Be back in a few."

Sarah slid into the break room and leaned against the doorway. Breathing hurt.

Everything inside her hurt.

She couldn't think the worst. Jude might not have been in that building. Even if he was, he could be just fine. She had to pull herself together. She had patients to see, had to get through the night no matter what happened.

She needed to get back out there because she

could hear nearing ambulance sirens wailing. Grabbing a cup, she filled it to the brim from the water dispenser, then downed it.

She needed something much stronger, but that would have to do.

She had this. Whatever the night brought. She had this.

Only when the doors opened and an elderly woman and a badly burned couple were rushed in, Sarah had to mentally brace herself.

The Millers and Betty Kingston.

No Jude.

Which probably meant that he was fine. He'd rescued them and was still there, fighting the fire.

Only Sarah's inside hurt and couldn't let go of the fear inside her.

Sarah and two other docs examined the new patients, taking over their care. Sarah had just gotten Mr. Miller ready to admit when there was another commotion as a group rushed in.

A group of firefighters carrying an unconscious Jude.

Sarah rushed over to the group, trying to get close enough to examine the man they carried.

"Bring him in here," she insisted, thanking God

that the transport crew had just come and emptied the room minutes before.

Shelley was there, wiping down the bed and throwing a clean sheet over it even as the men set Jude down.

Immediately, Sarah had oxygen on him, helped Shelley undress him to get telemetry hooked up. She flinched at the deep purplish bruises across his ribs, across his shoulder, but said a silent little thank you at the strong beep that filled the room with its reassuring sound.

"He insisted the three ambulances at the scene take the others, rather than him, that he'd wait until another showed up," one of the men she'd met at the fire hall said.

"When he lost consciousness, we decided there wasn't time to wait for another ambulance to show," Roger said, his gaze focusing in on what Sarah was doing and helping her get Jude situated on the bed as she cleaned a spot to start an intraosseous line. "So we loaded him up and brought him in the fire truck."

"Got him here faster than another ambulance could have gotten to us," another of the crew Sarah had met at the fire hall party piped up. "Much less have gotten him here."

Even while she listened to his crew tell about how Jude had gone rogue to rescue the Millers and had them almost out when another section of the building had caved in, she, Shelley and another nurse worked on him. They started the intraosseous line and got only a grunt from Jude.

That grunt was priceless, though, because it meant he had felt pain, that he was in there.

"He managed to clear a path to get them out by holding up a beam for the Millers to crawl beneath. After the couple had cleared the building, they were that close, he tried to clear himself of the beam to get out, but triggered another cave-in that trapped him beneath rubble."

"Roger there had tried to go back in the moment he had the Kingston woman out, but Command restrained him. There was no restraining any of us when the Millers came out and we realized he was trapped twenty feet or so from an exit."

Thank God Roger and whoever else of Jude's crew had gone back in.

His blood pressure was low, his pulse slightly

elevated. His oxygen was lower than it should be but not dangerously so. Yet.

Sarah gave another order to Shelley, preparing to establish an airway. She needed to get Jude stable, to be prepared for any scenario, so they could get scans to check for internal injuries in case of hemorrhage.

Please, don't let him be hemorrhaging.

Please, let him be okay.

Please, guide my hands and my mind as I do this.

Oh, God, how could she do this? How could she not? She didn't want anyone working on Jude other than herself. She needed to make sure everything possible was done, everything.

Sarah intubated Jude, not quite believing she was doing this to him. Her hands shook. She panicked just a little when the tube met more resistance than it should have. Mentally talking her way through what she was doing, she got the tube situated, sighing in relief when she checked placement and it was good.

Heartbeat low but steady. Airway established. Fluids going. Meds going.

Vitals stable for the moment.

She glanced around at the haggard, dirty crew who'd carried Jude into the emergency department. "I'm taking him for imaging to check for internal injuries and fractures. Other than insisting that he wait for the next ambulance, did he say anything particular before he went out? Mention somewhere he was hurting? That kind of thing?"

"We carried him out, but I don't think he'd broken anything. He'd had the air knocked out of him by the debris that fell on him."

"What kind of debris?"

"The big kind. Beams, ceiling tiles, dust, who knows what all that was? Visibility was next to nil and we were digging him out as quick as possible because the upper floors of the building were gone. We could hear explosions going off and although that ground floor wasn't on fire, the weight of everything above was pushing down hard and stuff was falling almost as fast as we could clear it.

"We cleared him of the building. Had him lying on the ground, but he was talking some. He kept saying your name."

She placed her hand over Jude's, squeezed the warmth she found there.

"He's going to be okay, isn't he?"
Sarah's gaze met Roger's. "He has to be."
Which said it all.

CHAPTER SIXTEEN

JUDE'S HEAD HURT. So did his body. But it was a strange hurt, almost as if he were experiencing the pain from somewhere far away from reality.

Breathing wasn't easy and his lungs felt full of dust and smoke.

The smoke put hazy thoughts into his head. Hazy thoughts of being in a burning building, weighed down in his gear. No, it wasn't his gear weighing him down. It was the building itself.

On top of him.

He couldn't move.

He tried to call out for help, but words wouldn't come. He tried to call for Sarah. He needed to tell her he was sorry, to tell her he wouldn't let their last conversation be an argument, as it had been with Nina. But no words sounded. Nothing. Just silent screams in his head.

Nina was there, too. Holding her hand out to him, telling him to come with her.

His voice wouldn't work or he'd have told her he didn't want to go. Not with her. His place was beside Sarah.

His heart belonged to Sarah.

He tried to tell Nina but smoke choked him, gagging him, making him feel as if he couldn't breathe.

But he must be because his chest was rising and falling. He could see it doing so, felt the pain with every expansion of his chest.

Even in his fog he realized he shouldn't be able to see himself, shouldn't be seeing the rise and fall of his chest. Yet he did.

He was lying in a hospital bed. His eyes were closed. He wasn't moving other than that chest rise and fall.

But he wasn't causing that excruciating rise and fall.

A machine breathed for him.

Somewhere in the fog he knew that should alarm him, but instead his attention went to the group huddled around him. His work family. Each and every one of them.

And Sarah.

Then they were all gone and a loud noise spun around him, sounding as if it was closing in on him.

Above that, Nina's voice came to him, calling him again.

"Sarah." He tried to answer, but couldn't. He went to reach for his throat to find out why he couldn't speak, but couldn't move his hands.

Nina's voice grew louder, beckoning him.

The radiology crew got the computerized tomography scans and X-rays and had Jude back in an emergency room bay in record time. Sarah stayed at his side except for the few minutes he was in the CT machine and then she waited next to the tech, ready to act if anything changed on Jude's vitals.

She'd consulted Pulmonology to assess his lungs. Neurology to assess his lack of consciousness. And wished she had a dozen more specialists to check him over in case she'd missed something. Logically, she'd gone over everything she knew to go over, was trying to look for any unknowns, and now it was a waiting game. If he stayed stable, she'd eventually have to transfer his care to the intensive care unit, but until she had to, she planned to keep him as close as possible.

The imaging tests showed no internal bleeding but lots of swelling and contusions. His chest images also showed that he'd fractured two ribs when the debris had fallen on him. Fortunately, they weren't displaced and hadn't punctured a lung or caused any significant soft-tissue damage.

"Thank you for what you're doing for him, Sarah."

She glanced over at where Roger stood, looking dirty, exhausted, ready to drop. Actually, all the fire crew did. No wonder. They'd gone from fighting fires and rescuing people to rushing one of their own to the emergency room.

"Roger, I'm going to take you guys to a private waiting area. It's actually where Jude waited the night we met when he'd brought in a little girl he rescued."

"I remember," Roger said. "But if it's all the same to you, we'd like to stay here with him."

"I understand. At least let me see if I can rustle up some chairs and some drinks, then."

"That would be great."

Sarah turned to go in search of vacant chairs and bottled drinks, but when she let go of Jude's hand, he grabbed her hand back.

"Oh," she gasped, shocked at the movement. Thrilled at the movement. "Did you see that?" she asked of no one in particular. "He moved."

"That he did, Doc. I think he wants you to stay right where you are. I tell you what," Roger said. "If you'll send us in the right direction we'll take you up on that drink and maybe a bathroom where we could wash up a little."

"Of course. Get the nurse who was in here earlier. Shelley. She'll take care of everything."

Roger nodded, then touched Jude's upper arm. "Wake up, my brother. I had a hot date tonight and I'm late, thanks to that fire and your nap."

Jude's hand jerked against hers and a noise came from somewhere deep in his chest as the crew each said something to Jude before leaving the room.

Sarah's eyes watered at the bond between them.

When she was alone with him, Sarah laced her fingers with Jude's. "Jude? Do you hear me? It's Sarah."

His hand jerked against hers again. For a moment she wondered if his movement was reflexive rather than intentional. However, when he squeezed her hand in a few rhythmic pulses her heart soared.

Intentional. Thank you, God, intentional.

"Jude," she said, fighting to keep her voice clear as tears almost choked her. "This is Sarah. You're in the emergency room. If you hear me, open your eyes."

Nothing.

She squeezed his hand a little tighter than normal. "Open your eyes for me, Jude."

He squeezed back again.

Sarah pulled her hand away so she could do a quick neuro check to see if he reacted to stimuli.

Pulling out a sharp point from her scrub pocket, she pressed it against his fingertip. Jude grimaced. Sarah smiled. She'd not gotten any response when she'd checked him prior to his imaging tests.

She ran through several other neuro tests, getting reactions to each one, then moved on to the one she'd been saving for last. Mainly because looking into his eyes earlier and seeing nothing but a blank stare had almost sent her into sobs.

She pushed his eyelids open, stared into the most beautiful blue eyes she'd ever gazed into and shone her light. As before, they responded appropriately to light, but he wasn't seeing her.

Or maybe he was because his stare wasn't blank. Not like before.

Jude saw her.

Some might think it was her imagination or wishful thinking but she knew better. Jude was seeing her.

She leaned closer, her face about six inches above his. "It's time for you to wake up, Jude Davenport. Do you hear me? Wake up."

Jude heard Sarah. Loud and clear. She was telling him to wake up.

Which didn't make sense because he was awake.

"Wake up, Jude," she insisted, louder.

His throat hurt. So did his head. And his body. He hurt all over.

"You know, tonight has been a really sucky one for me. First, you act like a total jerk at Charles and Grace's party. Then we argue and you break my heart. As if that isn't enough, you have the nerve to show up in my emergency room unconscious and I have to be nice to you. That's really not fair when I just want to not like you."

They'd argued.

Sarah had told him goodbye.

She wanted to not like him.

His heart hurt to go along with everything else.

He and Sarah had argued. He had to tell her he was sorry—tell her he hadn't meant to break her heart.

"And your crew are all worried and refusing to leave. You sure you aren't just playing possum to get attention?"

Jude tried to say her name, thought he might have, but she didn't respond if he had. Great. He'd try again, but couldn't because of his throat.

He reached up, pulled at the tubes.

"Stop that," Sarah ordered. "I worked hard to get that in place."

Sarah had done that to him?

His hand fell away.

And his eyes opened.

She was right there in front of him. Mere inches from his face. Sarah.

Sarah's breath caught. Jude was awake, was looking at her, tracking her with his eyes, seeing her.

He was seeing her!

"Hello, there," she whispered, not caring that tears streamed down her face.

He wanted to say something back, but couldn't, seemed irritated at the ventilator tubing. She glanced at his oxygen saturation. With the vent delivering oxygen, he was satting at ninety-nine percent.

She wanted to take the vent out.

If she did and he wasn't ready, she'd have to put it back in, would be risking injury, might not be able to re-establish an airway and would never forgive herself.

But truth was if it had been anyone else, she'd have pulled him off the vent already because she didn't think he needed it. Not anymore.

Maybe he never had, but she hadn't been willing to risk not maintaining an airway.

"I'm going to pull the vent, Jude. Don't you dare make me regret doing so," she ordered, gloving up and pulling the tubing from him.

He groaned during the removal, but sighed once he was free of the tube.

His hand went to his throat and rubbed the area as if that would somehow help.

"Your throat is going to be scratchy and sore for a while from the tube," she warned, as she put oxygen on him.

"Sarah."

Her hoarse name on his lips weakened her knees. "You shouldn't be talking. Just be quiet and use your energy to get better."

He shook his head, put his hand to his throat, and hoarsely whispered, "I'm sorry."

"Hey, Sarah, I put those firefighters— He's awake!" Shelley stopped short just inside the emergency room bay.

"Yes." Straightening from where she'd leaned closer to him, Sarah forced herself into professional mode, doing another quick neuro examination, checking sensation and movement and reflexes.

Other than obvious intense pain with movement, all good.

"If you wanted to play with my feet—" his voice was raspy, but understandable "—you could have just told me you had a foot fetish."

Sarah rolled her eyes. "You wish."

He cleared his throat. "I do."

That had her pausing in her examination. "You wish I had a foot fetish?"

His gaze bored into hers. "That you had a me fetish."

Sarah's breath caught. Shelley, who was still in the room, cleared her throat from the other side of the gurney where she checked lines.

"You've had a rough night, Jude," Sarah reminded him, trying to shake off all the emotions bombarding her. "You should focus on breathing deeply and not talking. Really. Just be quiet and breathe."

"Breathing hurts."

"Try not to and what I'll do to you will hurt a lot worse," she warned in the sternest tone she could muster.

"Mouth to mouth?"

"There you go wishing again. I'll shove that tube down your throat again and this time I won't be so gentle," she threatened. "So be quiet and conserve your energy for more essential things, like breathing deeply."

"I take it you two know each other?" Shelley asked as she jotted down numbers from his telemetry.

"He's my neighbor," Sarah explained.

At the same time Jude said, "We're dating."

Sarah's gaze cut to Jude. "In case you forgot, whatever was between us ended earlier tonight."

"What's between you and I hasn't ended. Never will." His oxygen monitor beeped, indicating his oxygen saturation had dropped below ninety percent.

Concern filled Sarah. She needed to focus on his health, not be having a personal conversation with him. He shouldn't be talking at all.

"Jude, please, stop," she pleaded, adjusting his oxygen tubing. "Just stop talking and breathe deeply or I really will put the vent back in."

"I could make a corny joke about you taking my breath away if it would help," he offered.

"You taking a deep breath would help. Several deep breaths." Sarah turned to Shelley. "Go tell his crew he's awake and they are welcome to come back in here so long as they can keep him quiet."

Shelley nodded and went to get his coworkers.

Jude sucked in a deep oxygen-rich breath, grimaced in pain, no doubt triggered by his fractured ribs and bruised chest. Then he took another, and another. His oxygen saturation instantly rose and Sarah sighed with relief.

"I tell you I'm sorry, that I don't want to say goodbye to you ever, and you tell me to breathe?"

She took a deep breath herself, then blew it out

slowly. "You don't know what you're saying, Jude. You suffered multiple injuries, were unconscious for who knows how long. You're not yourself."

"Then who am I?"

"Injured. Tired. Confused."

"I need you in my life."

She needed him, too. So very much, but it wasn't enough. Would never be enough. Not knowing what she knew.

"I can't do this, Jude. Maybe you don't understand, but I won't be second best. Not even to a dead woman."

Proving just how quickly he was recovering now that he'd regained consciousness, Jude scooted up in the bed.

"Have you not heard anything I've said?" His voice was still scratchy but getting stronger. "You are not second best. You are best. You, Sarah. You and only you. There is no second best."

Fresh tears ran down her cheeks. "Please, don't."

"Don't tell you how much I need you? That had we not been interrupted earlier tonight I'd have told you at your apartment? That I've known from the very first night, here, that you were special? That I wanted you to know you were different from anyone I'd ever known? Which don't do you mean?"

"I… But Nina…"

"Nina was an amazing woman, but I'm not in love with Nina." At Sarah's open mouth, he held up his hand. "Hear me out. Maybe I was always more in love with the idea of Nina and I than I was with Nina to begin with. Or maybe I didn't want to acknowledge what a jerk I was to her after she chose Charles. I don't know. What I do know is that when I thought I was taking my last breaths, I didn't want Nina. I wanted you, Sarah. Just you. Always you."

Trying not to let his words poke too many holes in her shabby defenses against him, she arched her brow. "This isn't some traumatic brain injury talking nonsense that you're not going to remember tomorrow?"

"I loved you before I left your apartment, before I made love to you last night. I think I loved you even before I took you to see your first Broadway show."

Sarah's jaw dropped and she grabbed hold of the bed railing to steady herself. "You love me?"

"I've never felt the way I feel about you. Not for Nina. Not for anyone. Just you."

His words sounded too good to be true.

"How do you know what you're feeling is real?"

"Because I feel it with every beat of my heart. I feel you with every beat." He took her hand into his and placed it over his chest. "Feel it? Sa-*rah*. Sa-*rah*. Sa-*rah*," he said in unison with his heartbeat.

Eyes blurring at the enormity of what he was saying, at what he was doing, Sarah shook her head. "You're crazy."

"About you."

She fought back a major sniffle. "So I heard."

"Mr. Johnson?"

Despite the hot-poker pain that moving obviously caused to streak through his body, he lifted her hand to his lips and pressed a kiss there. "That's what I want, Sarah."

"You want Mr. Johnson?"

This time he shook his head. "I want what he and his wife have. I want that with you."

"I love you, Jude, but—"

"Thank God," he said, pulling her down to him

despite whatever pain and trauma her landing against him caused.

"I'm going to hurt you," she insisted, trying to pull away, certain she was going to do major damage that she'd never forgive herself for.

"Yes, you are. Stop trying to get away and kiss me."

"But—"

"No buts, Sarah. Just you and me. Forever."

That had her staring wide-eyed at him. "Forever? I thought you just wanted me through Christmas."

"Haven't you figured out the truth yet, Sarah? I want you *for* Christmas," he corrected. "Not through Christmas."

"A doctor under the tree, eh?"

"A fireman in your stocking."

A fireman in her stocking. She closed her eyes, let herself dream a little, imagining what if what he was saying was true.

When she opened her eyes, looked into his, the truth shone so clearly that she was the one needing to be told to breathe.

"Forgive me, Sarah," he said. "Let me spend the rest of my life making tonight up to you."

The rest of his life. Jude and her forever. It's what she saw in his eyes, what she felt in her heart.

Being careful to try not to hurt him, she pressed a kiss to his cheek. "I'm the one who should ask you to forgive me. I was so scared of getting hurt that I almost threw everything away."

"I wouldn't have let you," he assured her, cradling her against him. "What we have is too special. I'll always fight for you."

"I'm dreaming."

"Then dream that my body doesn't feel as if a building fell on it so I can do all the things to you that I want to be doing to you."

"A building did fall on you." She placed her hands on his cheeks and stared into his eyes. "Please, don't forget you said all this, Jude. I need you not to forget."

"I love you, Sarah. Yesterday, today, and tomorrow. I'm yours."

"Yeah, and we all heard him say it and will hold his sorry butt to it, right, guys?"

Sarah turned to see his crew standing just inside the bay.

Jude grinned at his guys. "You won't ever have

to. All she has to do is say she's mine and I'm the luckiest man alive."

"You are lucky to be alive," Roger corrected. "Two minutes more and you'd have been buried under the entire building. Not sure if you remember, but the whole thing came down."

"Thank you for getting me out."

"Wasn't just me." Roger gestured to the others in the room. "Guess we'll all be getting a chewing from Command."

"Won't be the first time," one of the other crew said.

"Won't be the last," Jude finished, then returned his gaze to Sarah. "Think you can put up with having these guys around constantly?"

Sarah looked into his amazing blue eyes and let herself drown in what she saw there, the need to love and be loved.

"I've told you I always wanted a big family."

Cheers went up from around the bed, but neither Sarah nor Jude looked at his coworkers or heard their teasing words.

They had eyes only for each other as Jude said, "Yeah, well, there's more than one way to give you that."

Sarah smiled, because she knew what he meant and looked forward to each and every moment of the rest of their lives.

Together.

Forever.

* * * * *